GLASS HOUSE

ANDREA FRAZER

Glass House

ISBN: 9781783754441

DRAMATIS PERSONAE

Residents of Fairmile Green

Catcheside, Vince and Nerys – Church Cottage, Smithy Lane

Eastwood, Robin – River View, Market Street

Fairchild, Roger and Rita – Woodbine Cottage, Smithy Lane

Innocent, Matt and Anthea – The Old Smithy, Smithy Lane

Jones, Gareth – Or Not 2B, Old Darley Lane

McMurrough, Chadwick – Glass House, High Street

Radcliffe, Bailey – McMurrough's partner, Glass House, High Street

Smallwood, Ellie and Ollie – Green Gates, Market Street

Sutherland, Gerald and Lucille – Riverbanks, Market Street

Trussler, Keith and Kim – Fairview, Market Street

Warren, Christopher and Christine – Myrtle Cottage, High Street

Westbrook, Dean – 2B, Old Darley Lane

Worsley, Darren – Lane House, Old Darley Lane

Chadwick's Chatterers Crew

Allencourt, Dominic – McMurrough's agent

Betteridge, Daphne – Programme researcher

Crouch, Melody – Script editor

Hunt-Davies, Desmond – Director

Summersby, Neil – Producer

Officials

DI Harry Falconer of Market Darley CID

DS Davey Carmichael of Market Darley CID

DC Chris Roberts of Market Darley CID

Sergeant Bob Bryant – desk sergeant

PC Merv Green – uniform division, Market Darley Police

PC Linda 'Twinkle' Starr – uniform division, Market Darley Police

Superintendent Derek 'Jelly' Chivers, Market Darley Police

Dr Philip Christmas – Forensic Medical Examiner – amongst his many other medical duties.

Heather Antrobus – nurse at Market Darley General Hospital

PROLOGUE

Fairmile Green was a visually unusual village for more than one reason. Not only had all the shops that formed its small commercial sector been saved from demolition about a decade ago, and sympathetically restored, thus presenting the casual shopper with two rows of parallel-facing establishments with thatched roofs and timbered walls, but they were now trading as such unexpected businesses as a burger bar, sandwich shop, and £1 shop.

Most surprisingly, it had a juvenile section of the local river Darle, unimaginatively named the Little Darle, running between these two rows of commercial establishments; well-protected, of course, due to health and safety regulations, but a magnet for inquisitive children and thirsty dogs. With this charming rivulet dividing the village, the main thoroughfare was almost the widest in Britain, although the western side was named Market Street, the eastern, High Street. However, it did create a marvellously open view for the houses that ran across the end of these, as Stoney Cross Road turned left at this point, and Smithy Lane, right, thus ending the length of the thoroughfare at the southern end.

This infant river, which gave so much character to the village centre, eventually ran off underground under the property at the end of its main street, under a house which had for years been known as The Orchards.

Behind each of its rows of shops there was a little yard; the Bear Pit Yard behind the western shops, and Darley Old Yard behind the eastern. The tiny hamlet of Darley,

1

long ago disappeared into the mists of time, was remembered thus, as only a minuscule commercial cul-de-sac in another village, and with Market Darley, a town that had survived to carry the name, only about two-and-a-half miles away in an east-north-easterly direction.

Its even tenor of life was disturbed by the annual summer influx of tourists who wanted to photograph its almost sickening quaintness, and Fairmile Green had also been reluctantly enlivened by extensive works being carried out on the largest house in the village – the one underneath which the Little Darle disappeared.

Although the landlord of The Goat and Compasses didn't mind the hustle and bustle of extra trade, the villagers resented this intrusion on the rhythm of their lives, and looked forward to the completion of the building work, and the return of the hordes of tourists and their attendant children back to school, come September.

The largest house in Fairmile Green stood at the southern end of the village and had, as mentioned, always been called The Orchards. This building had once owned the whole frontage across both Market Street and High Street but, at some time in the first part of the twentieth century, the owner at the time had sold off little parcels of land for which the relevant authority was only too glad to grant planning permission, not wanting the village to die, as so many others were doing.

Thus, the big house now shared this enviable view down the centre of the village with half a dozen other residences, that particular owner of The Orchards being canny enough to sell only shallow plots, and having the stroke of brilliance to build a wall across all of the new boundaries, sacrificing only a few of the trees that made up the magnificent orchard that had been established to the rear of the property, and after which it had been named.

The house was just a little bit too young to be a listed building, but old enough to be dilapidated, having stood empty for the best part of a decade. The first sign that it had been sold had appeared nearly a year ago. There had been no For Sale sign, nor had there been a Sold sign, but the name-plates on the gate and the front of the house had suddenly been noticed not to be there any more, and a contractor's sign had been erected in the front garden.

That was the signal that something was afoot, closely followed by what was a positive storm of activity, with vehicles belonging to a plethora of trades visiting; there had been plumbers, electricians, general builders, glaziers, landscape gardeners, professional designers, kitchen specialists, flooring specialists, and interior and exterior decorators, none of whom had been local.

The name of the new owner was the best kept secret for miles around, and the locals speculated that, if it was someone famous, then a lot of money must have changed hands to maintain this level of discretion, and this amount of renovation.

When the whirlwind of activity – which lasted for about four months – ceased, the delivery vans began to arrive, bearing the names of some very select retailers, on their sides. The new owner of The Orchards must have considerable funds to have ordered from such august names.

At last, just a month or two ago, the owner himself had turned up with a man in navy overalls who was there to fit the new name-plate for the front wall, which read, simply 'Glass House'. So that's who it was! News spread like wildfire. They were going to have Chadwick McMurrough living amongst them.

McMurrough was the current media darling, having won the television competition *The Glass House*, in which twenty people were housed in a building with glass external walls, and were filmed twenty-four hours a day. With the exception of the lavatories and bathrooms, everything they did or said was filmed, recorded, edited, then broadcast to a gullible public so that they would evict the candidates one-by-one.

The bias for the series that had been broadcast the previous year had been towards a flamboyant character who was openly and outrageously gay, with the name Chadwick McMurrough. He was outrageous not only in his opinions, but in his dress, and the outré colours and styles he wore made the editors and production team swing wildly in his favour as winner, manipulating the footage to achieve their goal.

After the programme finished, apart from the monetary award for winning such a puerile programme, McMurrough was given a short-term part in the country's favourite soap opera, *Cockneys*, and the press began to dub him 'the gay, multi-coloured thespian'.

So charismatic and bizarre was the winner, that he was offered his own chat show on one of the minor television channels in a late slot on Friday evenings. Not surprisingly, given the level of taste of the average viewer, it had become cult viewing, and McMurrough a celebrity, albeit probably a fleeting one.

The new name of the house was a mystery to anyone who had not seen the rear of the property, thought only to refer to the show that had made all this possible, but sight of the back wall revealed that its main constituent was glass; it wasn't just an homage to the show that had been his first '*milch* cow', but a means of fully enjoying the view of the orchard, for which McMurrough had secret plans.

The rear now boasted a slight extension which made it possible to have a balcony right across the back, behind which was the newly positioned master suite. This opened right out on to the balcony with multi-fold glass doors, and convincingly produced the feeling of the outside coming right into the house.

Similarly, downstairs, the new boundary of the ground floor had a similar window which, when open, gave the same effect to what Chadwick insisted on calling the lounge, much to Radcliffe's disgust. There was a slight break in this, and then yet another folding set of glass doors across the rear of the enormous kitchen/breakfast room.

At the front of the house where the dining room was situated, a huge picture window had been installed, and a specially made wooden-slatted blind hung suspended, ready to provide privacy when McMurrough entertained, although given his gregarious and extrovert character, he would probably not lower when entertaining, thus bringing back memories of his time in *The Glass House*, and his guests a taste of what it was like to be constantly on view.

To be thus displayed lifted McMurrough's spirits, as it was through this high visibility that he had made his current reputation and money, and he wished to continue with this style of life for as long as possible by being as eccentric as he could, to catch the imagination of the media. He definitely had hidden shallows.

He also had a hidden temper as well, as was publicly displayed on the day they moved in, arriving in a sporty little car behind a van that seemed to have brought their personal bits and pieces.

One item was long and thin, and was pulled from the van by Chadwick, only to have his new partner, Bailey Radcliffe, round on him in anger. 'Mind how you handle that. It's got my rods in it. You know I want to take advantage of being out in the countryside to do a bit more fishing. It'll give you a bit of time to yourself for your first love – yourself.'

The couple had become an item when McMurrough was doing his short stint in *Cockneys*, as Radcliffe was one of the directors, and they had appeared a thoroughly odd couple given how many years – nay, decades – older than

McMurrough was this new beau. After so many years 'in the business', he was totally unfazed by his younger partner's current celebrity and carried on his rant without even pausing for breath.

'And don't you dare touch my fly cases. The last time you picked up one of those, it was in a terrible muddle when I opened it up. I can't think what you did with it – treated it as a maraca and gave it damned good shake?'

'Oh, unpack it your damned self,' replied Chadwick, storming off up the garden path and going into the house in a huff.

Chapter One

Monday
Market Darley

It was high summer, and the whole country seemed to be drowning in children. The streets were awash with them to such an extent that they spilled, with their parents, by necessity, it seemed, into what had previously been quiet havens of sanctuary, pub gardens and other usually 'adults only' areas.

Their mass release from their hitherto enforced studies had turned these preciously peaceful havens of privacy and tranquillity into places akin to bear-gardens, and there was no escape from their shrill and irritating presence. Thus thought DI Harry Falconer, this beautiful summer's day as he made his way back from lunch, via the bakery, to his office.

He felt as though he were wading waist-deep through a sea of dwarves, feeling as though he were part of a fairy-tale, but probably not one with a happy ending. Before the schools reopened at the end of the long summer holidays, there would, no doubt, have been several incidents either involving or caused by this river of short humanity.

He had nipped out for a ploughman's lunch today, in anticipation of the return of his DS, 'Davey' Carmichael, who had been on sick leave for so long it felt like for ever, after a near-fatal attack on him during a previous case a couple of months before.

Falconer had struggled through this time with a temporary replacement, DS Ngomo and for a short while, in the absence of DC Roberts, recovering from acute appendicitis, PC Merv Green was temporarily elevated to a plainclothes DC, much to his fiancée, PC 'Twinkle' Starr's, delight. She had ambitions for her man, and these did not include staying in uniform for the rest of his working life.

Ngomo was now safely back where he belonged and in the past, Merv had gone back into uniform, much to his secret delight, and Carmichael was coming back this afternoon.

Although Falconer had visited his colleague when he was in hospital, and many times since he had returned home to recuperate from his dreadful injury, he felt strangely nervous about resuming their partnership.

The attack on Carmichael had focused the inspector's mind on his attitudes to life and people, and had made him more human, more emotional and, ultimately, more vulnerable. He must not wrap Carmichael in cotton wool. The attack had been a dreadful stroke of bad luck for which Falconer had no need whatsoever to feel guilty, and he mustn't think it was about to happen again.

Fairmile Green

'Peacocks?' queried Bailey Radcliffe, his voice rising at the idiocy of the idea. '*Peacocks*? You bought some *peacocks*? You actually *bought* some peacocks? What do *you* know about bloody peacocks, dipstick?'

'Oh, shut your face, you old queen,' replied Chadwick McMurrough to his partner of several weeks now. 'I've always wanted some, from when I was little, and now I can afford them. So I bought some, OK?'

'No, it's not OK,' Radcliffe snapped back at him. 'Do you realise the noise the damned things make? And what do they eat? Do you know how to look after them?'

'Of course I don't, but I can look it up on the internet, and if you don't like the noise you can always wear earplugs. Anyway, I've sent the delivery guy round to the orchard where he can let them out, and we'll just have to see how it goes. He's brought a little wooden house as well, for them to sleep in, or something.'

As he finished speaking, a high-pitched cry of what sounded like 'help' sounded from the rear of the house, and Radcliffe stared at his younger partner with an 'I told you so' expression on his face.

'See, stupid, you can even hear them through double glazing.'

'I see what you mean,' agreed McMurrough, and then added doubtfully, 'I suppose we'll get used to it. Eventually. Is it just swans that only the Queen's allowed to eat, or does the rule apply to peacocks too?'

'Well, if they get on my wick sufficiently, *this* queen's going to eat the little sods. No doubt you paid a fortune for them, too?'

'It's my money.'

'Well, maybe you need some therapy before you buy anything else daft. I don't want to get back here one day and find the garden full of bloody giraffes and the like.'

'Don't be ridiculous. Why would I want giraffes?'

'Maybe you fancied them, too, when you were little, or maybe you thought they'd keep the tops of the fruit trees tidy. How would I know? You've got such a weird mind.'

'Hmph!' McMurrough made a gruesome face at his significant other and flounced out of the room to view his new acquisitions, calling back over his shoulder, 'You wait to see what's next,' in a triumphant tone of voice.

Market Darley

Falconer had left DC Roberts back at the office blowing up balloons, and Merv and PC Starr hanging a 'welcome home' banner. His job was to collect a tray of cream cakes from the bakery in the market square and convey it back to complete the preparations for Carmichael's return, and these he now conveyed up the stairs to the CID office, ready for the hero's welcome that his sergeant so richly deserved after all he had been through in the last few months.

The banner had been affixed so that it was the first thing the DS would see when he came through the door, and the two PCs had vacated the room for the canteen, to have a little light lunch before attacking the pastries a little later. Roberts was surrounded by balloons, but they were on the floor, lying like a clutch of multi-coloured aliens' eggs, instead of tied into small groups and affixed to the ceiling. Roberts himself was slumped over his desk huffing and puffing as if he had just run a marathon.

'What the hell's the matter with you, and why aren't these things strung up?' barked Falconer, his temper, as always with Roberts, as short as a winter's day.

'I'm wiped out with all that blowing up, guv'nor,' replied Roberts, playing for sympathy he was never likely to elicit from this particular source. 'I think I may be developing asthma.'

'What did you just call me?' asked Falconer, ignoring the DC's plight.

'Sorry. Sir!' replied Roberts, realising he was on to a loser here. 'I'll just get the string and tape and get it finished.'

'You'd better. He'll be here in a few minutes. Get a move on! And no stringing one long one with two round ones and going for the "are-they-really-rude, I-simply-

10

didn't-realise" look. And there's no more sick leave for you for the next ten years after all the time you've taken off since you came here. I want to make that crystal clear.'

'You can't accuse me of swinging the lead. I was in hospital on all three of those occasions,' replied Roberts in a hurt voice.

'So you say,' said Falconer acidly.

Fortunately, they were interrupted at that moment, by the sound of cheering from downstairs, and the sound of a number of feet on the stairs. 'He's here!' declared Falconer, beaming from ear to ear and forgetting about his beef with the DC.

The less colourful – sometimes – brother of the Jolly Green Giant loped into the room with a beam of pure pleasure to be back where he belonged, and Falconer rushed forward to pump his hand so hard that Carmichael winced, and suddenly the office was bursting with people, all welcoming back one of their own, who had come so close to losing his life in service to the Force.

By the end of the afternoon, everything felt back to normal and, as Falconer drove home, he suddenly remembered he was having dinner with a friend on Wednesday evening, a fact he had completely forgotten in his preoccupation with Carmichael's return.

Once a fortnight he shared an evening meal with Heather Antrobus, a nurse he had met while visiting his DS in hospital. She had been involved in his day-to-day nursing, and she and Falconer often met by the sergeant's bedside. They also crossed paths in the hospital canteen where Falconer often ate when visiting, and she was trying to catch a brief meal-break.

Inevitably, they had talked about her patient, and he found her both intelligent and possessed of a sense of humour that was just about identical to his own. She was half-Irish, short, and a little on the plump side, with copper

11

beech-coloured hair and impish green eyes, and he enjoyed her company enormously.

When Carmichael had been discharged to convalesce at home, she and Falconer had agreed to meet outside duty hours whenever possible, for a simple supper and agreeable conversation, and he looked forward eagerly to these occasions. Not only did they distract him from bitter memories of a woman who had entered his life briefly and almost destroyed it, but he always felt on top of the world afterwards, putting this down to the good laugh they always shared with these meals.

Fairmile Green

McMurrough and Radcliffe were sitting in the drawing room of Glass House with the television blaring loudly in the corner to try to block out the cries of their new charges, or rather, as Radcliffe preferred to think of them, as Chadwick's latest little follies.

He was aware that his partner had already realised that maybe he'd made a tiny error of judgement by locating these screaming monsters on his own property, but he was as stubborn as a mule, and it would be some time before he got around to admitting he had made a mistake.

'Come along, Dr Doolittle,' Radcliffe shouted, above the unholy racket of the television at loud volume, in competition with the peacocks establishing their new territory. 'Let's go down the pub. At least with the fruit machines, video games, and jukebox it'll be quieter down there.'

'Point taken,' replied McMurrough. 'Although we haven't actually been inside it to see what it's like, yet.'

'Well, this feels like just the right opportunity to find out. Get your shoes on and we'll mince down there. I'll just nip upstairs and change my shirt, and I'll meet you outside.'

The Goat and Compasses was right at the other end of the High Street, and as they strolled down to it they could still hear the cries for help from the back of Glass House. 'This isn't going to endear you to the neighbours,' opined Radcliffe, and with a sorrowful shake of the head, McMurrough had to agree with him, although he still asserted his right to keep whatever pets he chose to.

The pub had no jukebox, no video games, and no fruit machines and was, in fact, a haven of calm. It was only early evening and there were few customers. The tables outside were deserted, but the couple chose to drink inside, where the incessant high-pitched cries were inaudible.

The interior was just what a village pub should be, with shining horse-brasses, copper pots and pans, and a variety of pint pots belonging to regulars, hanging up behind the highly polished bar. They didn't manage more than a couple of gin-and-tonics each before they were thoroughly rattled by the complaints of every customer who came in, having a good old moan with the landlord about the mysterious cries that were now audible from every corner of the village.

What the two new arrivals had failed to notice was that those already present in the bar, and those that arrived after them, gave the newcomers a long, hard, staring at, then went into little huddles of two or three, commenting in lowered tones on the 'odd couple' who were drinking in the corner.

'Have you seen the colours that younger one's wearing? A pink shirt and custard yellow trousers aren't, in my opinion, suitable for a nice respectable pub like this. And I'm sure I know his face from somewhere, but I can't put my finger on where.'

'That older one's wearing a toupee. That's completely undignified, if you know what I mean. Me, I just run the

13

razor over mine when I'm shaving. There's nothing wrong in being bald.'

'Aren't they the ones that have moved into The Orchards?'

'Oh, it's not called that any more. That name mustn't have been good enough for them. They've got a new sign with "Glass House" on it; a big one – etched glass or something similarly fanciful, as if wood wasn't good enough for them, like it is for the rest of us!'

The two residents of the village, aware only of the complaints about the noise, which were not spoken quite *sotto voce*, sipped their drinks, oblivious to these other complaints expressed in more hushed tones.

Returning home before dusk, they entered the house only to find a peacock in the hall, and peacock shit on the brand new white shag-pile carpet. The first verbal response was from McMurrough, who said shamefacedly, 'Oh God, I'm sorry!'

'This is down to you, is it?' asked Radcliffe, wrinkling his nose in distaste.

'I went outside to scatter some of that feed that was brought with them when you were upstairs changing your shirt,' he explained. 'I must have left the wall open.' This wasn't as daft as it sounded, for what would have been patio doors in any other house, were extremely over-sized in this one, to aid the illusion of a glass wall.

'You mean they've been able to get in since we went out?' asked his partner, aghast.

''Fraid so. Sorry.'

'You will be. They've probably crapped all over the place. I just hope they're no good at doing stairs: terrible stain to shift, peacock poo.'

'Is it?' asked McMurrough with horror.

'How the hell should I know? I've never had peacocks

in my life, but I bet the stains are just about indelible. Now, I'll get those doors shut and locked, and you can check there aren't any of those superannuated chickens upstairs doing ghastly things in our room.'

As Radcliffe closed and locked the huge doors, there was a thump, and a series of thuds accompanied by a scream.

Market Darley

Falconer got a call from Bob Bryant at the station about ten o'clock, informing him that there had been what the caller described as 'an attempt on his partner's life', out at Fairmile Green. The partner was some sort of celebrity and, after disturbing Superintendent Chivers at home, he had been advised to use senior officers, and not send out uniformed PCs. 'Jelly', as he was known, was very sensitive to anything media-related, and was wary of being portrayed in a bad light, if he didn't send someone of sufficient rank to attend the incident.

Taking down the address as Glass House, High Street, Fairmile Green, Falconer gave Carmichael a call, just to check that he was feeling up to going out late in the evening. If not, he would have to take Roberts, and he didn't fancy that one little bit; certainly not with a celebrity involved, as Roberts would probably be star-struck and do something embarrassing like ask for an autograph.

Carmichael was, however, feeling fit and raring to go. He'd been bored out of his mind during his convalescence, and couldn't wait to get involved with a new case. 'Are you OK to drive?' asked Falconer, beginning to behave like a mother hen. It was only a trip of two-and-a-half miles for him, but more like ten for Carmichael.

'Of course I'm OK to drive. How do you think I got to

the station today? Give me the address and a ten-minute start, and I'll meet you outside the property.'

After a minute or two, Falconer found that he could not face another eight minutes of pacing the floor getting paranoid about something else happening to his sergeant, and set off early; thus he was already parked up when Carmichael's battered and rusting old Skoda pulled out of Stoney Cross Road and crossed Market Street to where the inspector's Boxster was already waiting for him.

As the two men locked their cars, Falconer said, 'I must have got here quicker than I anticipated,' not only to make Carmichael think he'd only just arrived, but to cover his own embarrassment at being such a worry-guts. It would never do for Carmichael to realise his boss was turning into an old woman.

'It looks like this place has had a bit of work done on it,' commented the younger man, as Falconer rang the bell, then started with surprise as the clearly recognisable but, at present, unidentifiable theme tune of a television programme rang out in tinkling form.

The door was answered by a man somewhere in his late forties or early fifties wearing a good, but not that good, wig, and an expression that denoted extreme anxiety. Without preamble, this study in fear informed them, 'They must have got in when we were down the pub. Forget-Me-Not forgot to close the back doors, and anyone could have got in. It's a miracle we weren't cleaned out at the same time, but setting a booby trap was just spiteful.'

'Why don't we go inside, and we can talk about whatever's happened a little more calmly,' suggested Falconer, moving to insert his foot over the door jamb.

'Oh, where are my manners,' replied the, for the moment, unidentified man in the toupee, and preceded them into a sumptuous drawing room, the back wall of which was almost entirely made of glass.

'Nice place you've got here,' commented Falconer, while Carmichael just stood, his mouth agape, catching flies.

'Nice of you to say so,' replied their host. 'By the way, I'm Bailey Radcliffe, and my partner, Chadwick McMurrough, is upstairs having a little lie down. It was he, you see, who was the victim of this attempted murder.'

'Chadwick McMurrough?' squeaked Carmichael. '*The Glass House*? *Cockneys*? *Chadwick's Chatterers*?'

'That's right. Are you a fan?' Radcliffe was interested to find out. He was much more at ease now the cavalry had arrived.

'He really makes me laugh,' replied Carmichael, his face breaking out into a wide grin. 'I've been in hospital, then convalescing at home, and his programme was one of the things that kept me sane. He asks such outrageous questions, and the looks on his guests' faces when he does is priceless.'

It was now Falconer's mouth that gaped open in surprise that his sergeant should watch such candyfloss pap.

They were almost immediately distracted, however, by the pattering of slippered feet down the stairs, and Chadwick McMurrough, in the flesh, tripped – although not literally, this time – through the door, his face wreathed in smiles as he approached the policemen with his hand outstretched.

McMurrough, being the sort of person he was, had already crept down as soon as they had been admitted, and had been shamelessly eavesdropping, before creeping back to the landing, from whence he had descended for a second time, but with a slightly heavier tread.

Falconer shook the outstretched hand briefly, but Carmichael almost curtsied in honour, as he pumped the minor celebrity's hand for rather longer than appeared necessary or appropriate, as introductions were made.

'Shall we get down to business then, gentlemen?' queried Falconer, feeling slightly queasy at the hero-worship in Carmichael's eyes, and Radcliffe waved them towards a pair of white sofas that proved to be feather-stuffed, something that Falconer didn't discover until he sank so far down into one that his knees were almost round his ears. Carmichael looked even more ridiculous, given his enormous height.

McMurrough took one look at the sergeant and said, a wicked smile lighting up his face, 'My, they breed 'em big round here for the Force, don't they? Tell me, are there any more at home like you?'

Although Carmichael was married now and had two step-children and one of his own, his mind still flew back to the chaotic over-crowded nest that had been his childhood home.

Carmichael merely gulped, then croaked, 'Yes. Lots,' in reply, thinking how jealous his brothers, and possibly his sisters too, would feel when they found out that he had met – actually met – the famous Chadwick McMurrough.

Radcliffe interrupted, saying, 'Don't tease the poor man, Chaddy. He's not used to you and your wicked comments,' but McMurrough, so easily distracted, was now watching with great enjoyment how Carmichael was going to be able to manipulate his pen and notebook, when his knees were higher than his nose.

'Would you care to sit in a more upright chair?' asked Radcliffe with a sigh of exasperation, as he watched McMurrough snicker behind his hand at the incongruous sight of what looked like a stork trying to take notes.

Carmichael finally settled on an upright, very trendy, wooden chair. Falconer asked, with some frustration in his voice at the delay, 'Do you think we could get on with what actually happened.? I'm sure you gentlemen want to get off to bed as much as we do,' then blushed a rich crimson as he examined, in retrospect, what he had just said, conscious of a hastily suppressed snigger from McMurrough, who had also seen the interpretation that could be applied to the inspector's words.

'Shut up, Chaddy, and leave the poor policemen alone. I'll do the talking, for now, if you don't mind, Mr Gobby.'

They got no further than this before there was a cry of 'help' in a female pitch of voice, from the garden, and Carmichael shot up from his chair and raced to the rear glass doors, scrabbling at the mechanism to open them.

'Leave it, Sergeant,' advised Radcliffe with a sigh of exasperation. 'It's only a peacock. They do sound awfully human, but it was soft lad here's idea to get them, so he can work out what to do with them. They're driving me out of my mind already, and they only arrived earlier today.'

Carmichael re-took his seat, his face now as red as the inspector's, at this monumental gaffe. What did he know of peacocks? They were moving in high circles here, and no mistake. When he'd set off for the station just after lunch, he had had no idea he'd be hobnobbing with a celebrity before bedtime.

'Now, I'll tell this,' began Radcliffe, with a glare at McMurrough, 'up to the time that our little victim fell down the stairs, then it's up to you what you want to do about it, Officers. We went out for a drink earlier, to get away from the awful sound from out back. Just before we left, I went upstairs to change my shirt, not knowing soft lad here had gone out into the garden to throw some food for those screaming monsters. Guess who forgot to close the doors properly and lock them?

'We didn't discover this until we got back, and all seemed to be well, so we locked up, and my significant other here went trotting off upstairs. The next thing I knew there was this awful girly scream, and he bounced down the whole flight like a lead balloon, a positive rainbow in motion.

'Once I'd got him on his feet and given him his dummy dipped in gin to pacify him, I had a look to see what he'd stumbled over, and there was a trip-wire stretched across the staircase, two steps down from the top. It could only have been put there while we were out at the pub, and only be made possible because Chaddy forgot to lock up.

'To my mind, that indicates that we were being watched, and the fact that whoever it was, was able to get in, was just by the purest bad luck, for us – or rather, for him over there; the one covered in bruises, I don't think! Any ideas how we go about tracking down whodunit?

'To my mind, this was no practical joke. He could easily have been killed, or broken his neck and been paralysed. And, with such a serious attempt to harm him, I'm pretty positive that whoever it is will try again.'

'I'll get someone over to dust for prints and look for any sign of an intruder in the rear garden. We'll also need your fingerprints for elimination purposes – I'm sure you understand why.

'I can also increase the frequency with which a patrol car passes through the village, making sure that they have an extra good look at the exterior of your property, but apart from that, there's nothing else we can do. There simply isn't the manpower to put someone on permanent guard,' said Falconer glumly, hoping that this so-called celebrity didn't use his fifteen minutes of fame to set the press on to them.

'Well, I suppose that'll have to do, for now, but if there's any further nonsense – maybe injury – I shall have to get on to a private security firm for protection. In the meantime, I'll get Chadwick to order the installation of CCTV coverage of the outside, so that if anything else occurs, we'll at least have some evidence to put forward.'

Radcliffe was sounding the most serious he had since he had bidden the policemen enter the house, and McMurrough merely sat in thoughtful mood, gently rubbing his bruises, as his partner ushered Falconer and Carmichael out of the house.

Back beside their cars, Carmichael was also looking introspective, and when Falconer asked him what he was thinking about, he replied, 'I'm just glad I'm not famous, that's all.'

Chapter Two

Tuesday
Fairmile Green

At Glass House, there was a ring on the doorbell at eight-thirty the next morning, catching both inhabitants still in bed, and necessitating Radcliffe to run downstairs in his dressing gown and slippers, for McMurrough would no more have volunteered to go down to answer it himself than fly to the moon.

On the doorstep, stood two men in smart bottle-green uniforms, one man positioned slightly behind the other. Radcliffe had no idea that he was witnessing a well-rehearsed delivery pattern, and just stood there, dumbfounded, wondering what on earth this was all about.

'Good morning, sir,' intoned the man in front. 'PPP at your service this lovely morning, sir' As he said this, he thrust a large cardboard box into Radcliffe's arms, while his partner moved to the front, announcing, 'And here is the little precious himself: one miniature dachshund, for your enjoyment – registered name "Dipsy Daxie". If you'll just sign this receipt, sir, we wish you many happy years with your new pet.'

'What the hell's going on?' asked Radcliffe, as he hurriedly put the box on the ground to accept the wire cage that was thrust at him, a tiny form curled up inside it. And what the heck's PPP?' He'd signed the receipt and taken charge of the cage before he could gather his wits sufficiently to realise what he'd just done.

'Posh Pet Procurement, Mr McMurrough. Thank you for using our service,' replied the first man in explanation, then they both turned on their heels and walked off the property, got into their van, and drove off, leaving Radcliffe standing on the doorstep with a look on his face that declared that he had just been royally done over.

'CHADWICK!' he yelled, loud enough to waken the dead, or at least a very lazy partner. 'What the hell's this elongated rat you seem to have purchased for? Dinner?' and was not impressed when Chadwick came bounding down the stairs with the proud look of young motherhood on his face, making little kissing noises and crooning, 'Dipsy, darling, come to Daddy, and just ignore cross old Auntie Bailey.'

Auntie Bailey's face would have looked more at home in the Old Bailey, as a witness for the prosecution, especially when 'Dipsy darling' woke up and began to howl miserably at the absence of his mother and siblings.

'And if you think you're going to fob off walking that thing on me, you can think again. I will *not* – I repeat – I will *not* be seen in public exercising a saveloy on a lead. That thing looks like a cocktail sausage on four sticks.

'As far as I'm concerned, Dappy Dixie, or whatever the thing's called, is all yours. You're the one who's going to be feeding it, walking it, and bathing it. Me, I'm nothing to do with it. This is your toy, kid, and you can leave me right out of it. I've suddenly developed a severe allergy to dogs.'

'That's Dipsy Daxie, if you don't mind. Kindly remember his name, as he is now one of the family.' Chadwick had taken the little animal out of its cage and was cuddling it like a baby. 'Just you ignore nasty old Auntie Bailey; it must be the time of the month, he's such an old grump-pot.'

'And you can sort out the contents of that bloody great box as well. I'm not having that in the hall for a fortnight while you get round to it.' Bailey was working up quite a head of steam, in his indignation that his partner could have ordered such a thing – and after the peacocks, too – without a word of consultation, too – that he felt he could easily burst.

Characteristically, Chadwick ignored his partner's protests and sat down on the floor to unpack his goodie-box. 'Lead and collar; check. Feeding bowl and water bowl; check. Squeaky toys; check. Soft toys; check. Pooper scooper; check. Wicker basket and blanket for sleeping; check …'

'You haven't listened to a word I've said, have you, you little git,' Bailey protested crossly.

'Nope.'

At this cold-hearted and negative response, Bailey 'took his bum in his hands', threw open the multi-fold glass doors to the back garden, and went out in a huff, Chadwick's voice floating after him.

'And when you get back indoors, there's been enough talk about other things. I suggest we get back to me, and talk about something really interesting.' Bailey was back within two minutes, nursing a bloodied hand.

'What've you done, cut yourself on that sharp tongue of yours?' queried McMurrough, sarcastically. And shut the doors. 'My little treasure may get out before he's ready.'

'Damn your little treasure! One of your blasted peacocks has bitten me.'

'I believe you'll find that's "pecked". They don't have teeth.'

'And neither will you, if you don't start being just a little more civil,' his bloodied but unbowed partner

24

snapped and, with that, Bailey took himself upstairs to the first-aid kit, whereupon he found that Chadwick had opened to their fullest extent, the matching multi-fold doors in the master-suite at the rear of the house, and a fine collection of flying insects had taken advantage of the opportunity to come in and have a free viewing.

Wednesday
Market Darley

Falconer had thoroughly enjoyed the first of Carmichael's full days back in the office and would have appreciated it even more, had he known it would be his last peaceful day for quite a while. And this evening he was having dinner with Heather. Life was grand at the moment, and he didn't even consider this newly established even tenor not continuing. He dressed with care as a mark of respect for his companion, then picked her up from the nurses' home where she was staying while her flat in the Midlands was waiting to be sold.

They had a regular booking at a little Italian restaurant in the Market Square, flexible enough to allow for their respective jobs and the vagaries of the hours of these diverse but, in many ways, similar careers. Heather had nursed the owner's wife through a gallstone operation about six months ago, and he was still grateful for the way she had sat with her and coaxed her to eat, when she felt she'd never be able to face food again.

Their table was booked for seven-thirty, reasonably early, but it gave them half a chance of getting at least one course down their throats, before one of them was summoned on an unplanned call-out, and they had plenty to talk about tonight.

Heather had been involved in dealing with the victims of a multi-car pile-up on the road south into Market

Darley; the consequence, it seemed, of urban-dwelling tourists and their lack of experience on such narrow country roads, although to the locals, that particular road was judged to be a good-sized one. It happened at least once every summer, and when the first of last year's had occurred she had just started working at the hospital.

At the end of her tale, Falconer asked her if she knew when he had first noticed her at the hospital and, when she replied that she didn't, proceeded to describe the scene that had so caught his eye.

'You were standing at the bed next to Carmichael's, holding one of those pressed cardboard bowls, when the patient in the bed suddenly projectile vomited all down your front. Instead of being angry or disgusted, you just started laughing uproariously at your plight, eventually getting the patient to join in, at the state of your uniform.

'That was probably the best medicine you could have offered him; no apologies and embarrassment, just a damned good laugh. Then, when you leaned over to tear off some of that all-purpose hospital paper, I noticed a little ladder in the left leg of your tights just lengthen another half inch. I couldn't take my eyes off that tiny imperfection growing totally without your knowledge, and I realised I wanted to talk to you.'

'I remember the incident well, and we did seem to meet in the canteen quite frequently after that,' she replied.

'And by Carmichael's bedside,' he added.

'Which was *my* doing,' she chimed in. 'I rather wanted to get to know you too, as your visits seemed to do Davey so much good. I say, this carbonara's absolutely ace, isn't it?'

'I'll say. Are you going to have zabaglione for dessert? And I'll tell you what I've been up to.'

Having hailed the waiter and ordered their final course, he told her about Carmichael coming back to the office on

Monday night, yesterday being his first full day back in harness. 'You make sure you don't work poor Davey too hard. He's had a very bad time of it, as you well know, over the last couple of months.'

'"Poor Davey", as you insist on calling that great big lump, was thrilled to bits with the call-out we had Monday night.'

'You didn't get him out late, did you, you cruel beast? I told you, the boy needs his rest. You really are a slave driver.'

'He'd never have forgiven me if I hadn't taken him with me. The call was only to Chadwick McMurrough's house.'

'No!' she squeaked, not even giving him time to ask her if she'd ever heard of him. 'Not that brightly dressed camp guy with the chat show?'

'That's the one,' agreed Falconer.

'Ooh! I think he's lovely. I was rooting for him all the way through *The Glass House* and I watched him in *Cockneys*.' Here she paused as if in amusing memory. 'And I never miss one of his chat shows. If I'm on duty I have to record it; he's just so funny. I wish I could have gone with you; I'd love to meet him, although I'd probably die of embarrassment.'

'So, you're a closet Chadwick fan, are you?' asked Falconer, in surprise. This was exactly the sort of thing that happened when you only met up once a fortnight.

'Not exactly 'closet', and I had no idea he'd moved into the area. Where did you say he was?'

'Fairmile Green.'

Fairmile Green

'I'm going to take Dipsy for a little walk,' announced

27

Chadwick. 'You coming, Bailey?'

'Are you out of your tiny little mind?' his partner responded. 'When I said I wouldn't be seen dead with that mobile chorizo, I meant it. I'm going to have a little nap, then, when you get back, I might deign to accompany you to the local hostelry for a little liquid refreshment.

'If you're lucky, there might be some fans of yours there, and you can sit and bask in their admiration, before we come back here and retire for the night. That sort of thing always puts you in a good mood.'

'Suit yourself, sweetie, but I'm off.'

'I hope none of the neighbours dies laughing.'

'Bitch!'

'Silly cow! Have a nice walk with your mini-Cumberland.'

Radcliffe stretched himself out on the extra-long, white leather sofa and was asleep within minutes, his snoring, for once, unappreciated by either man or beast.

The next thing of which he was aware was the echo of what he immediately identified as a howl of pain, followed by some very rich and loud swearing, and a face appeared at the rear glass doors, filled with anguish.

Leaping to his feet and making a rush for the doors, he unlatched them and admitted Chadwick, clutching one shoulder with one hand, the other, limply clutching the lead of the tiny pup.

As Radcliffe grabbed the lead and pulled the dog inside, Chadwick began to groan with pain, and to insist that Bailey called the police once more and, if necessary, a doctor.

'What in the name of God has happened?'

'I decided to come in the back way so that Dipsy could do any business he needed to conduct in the garden before we came in, and maybe he'd not need to go while we're out. But when I opened the side gate, a bloody great stone, which must have been balanced on the top, fell off and landed on my shoulder. I'm sure it's broken.'

'Your shoulder would never break a stone. Where did you leave it? By the gate?'

'You unfeeling bitch!'

'Come here and let me see.'

'I'm in agony here, and all you can do is insult me,' replied McMurrough, stripping off his long-sleeved T-shirt to reveal a slight graze and a swelling that would turn, overnight, into quite a satisfactory bruise.

'You big baby! There's no way that's broken, but it looks pretty painful.'

'What if it had landed on my head?'

'Then the thickness of your skull definitely would have shattered it.'

'Cow! What if it had landed on Dipsy? It would have killed him.'

'That's true. I think you're right about reporting this. After that episode the other evening, we'd better just give the police a ring. Better safe than paying for a funeral.' Radcliffe was all heart. 'But you don't need to waste a doctor's time. All he'd do would be to send you for an x-ray. Do you really want to spend the evening hanging around in A&E?'

'No way, but you could ring me mum as well. I could do with a bit of TLC, and I'm not likely to get that from you in a million years,' requested McMurrough.

'Sod your mum. What's that stunted frankfurter doing on the new wooden floor. Hey, stop that this minute! And what are you looking so glum about?'

'It'll be too late to go to the pub if we have to wait for the police.'

'Tough, you spoiled little brat.'

Market Darley

While Heather was still cross-questioning Falconer about Chadwick McMurrough's new residence, his mobile phone rang, putting paid to the flow of questions for a few minutes. When he ended the call, he smiled at her and said, 'I've got to go over to Fairmile Green again. There's been another attack, albeit a minor one, on our nine days' wonder local celebrity. Would you care to accompany me?'

'You bet your life I would. Just hang on while I get the rest of this zabaglione down my neck, and we can get straight off,' replied, Heather, beginning to spoon her dessert into her mouth with almost unbelievable speed. 'There, finished. Let's go!' she announced, only to be stalled by her dinner partner, who chose to finish his at his leisure, calling for the bill and not rushing himself. Falconer was cool, or so he secretly believed.

'Take off your shoes,' ordered Heather, in a rather brusque manner, and quite inexplicably.

'Why on earth do you want me to do that?'

'So I can count your toes. At the moment I'd put money on you only having three – you sloth.'

Fairmile Green

Falconer hadn't bothered disturbing Carmichael over this call, and had informed Bob Bryant that he would go alone – at least technically alone – and Bob agreed with this decision. It didn't sound very serious, and the sergeant would need a bit more rest than usual, having just returned to work; and Falconer didn't even want to think about having to summon DC Roberts, not when his evening, thus far, had been delightful.

Radcliffe must have been watching out for the car from the dining room window, for the door was opened before the two of them had even got through the gate. 'Is it OK if my friend comes in?' asked Falconer, as they approached the front door, 'Only we were having supper when I received the call that you'd had another spot of bother.'

'No problem,' Bailey replied. 'We've already got Chadwick's ever-loving mother here: the more the merrier.' The man did not seem best pleased at the way the house was filling up. With these two, that would now make five adults, a ridiculously shaped puppy, and God knew how many fancy birds at the back.

In the lounge they found McMurrough, sitting mournfully on the over-sized sofa, his arm in a sling, his face like a wet weekend. 'Good evening, Mr McMurrough,' Falconer greeted him. 'I hope you don't mind, but I was in a restaurant having a meal with my friend when I got the call to come here, and it seemed churlish, if not time-wasting, not to come straight here.'

'Be my guest,' the invalid replied. 'You can see for yourselves what agony I'm in,' and he winced theatrically and put a hand to his injured shoulder. There didn't seem to be anyone else in the room, until a voice uttered from behind a large white leather armchair, its back to them, and facing a very large television set which burbled away quietly.

Above the sound of the television, the voice suddenly opined, 'Great big girl's blouse. Talk about making a mountain out of a molehill. But then you always were a jessie.'

At their expressions of surprise, McMurrough said, 'You haven't met my mother, have you? She's the one in front of the TV with a tray of blinis, cream cheese, smoked salmon, and caviar on her lap. Say 'hello', Mummy Dearest.'

31

Falconer and Heather took a few paces down the room and saw the middle-aged woman, sitting in the chair like a malignant goddess guarding her ambrosial snack. 'I made 'im three slices of toast, cheese, and tomato and a huge mug of 'ot chocolate,' the deity proclaimed, 'and that's all the TLC 'e's getting from me for one night. From the phone call, I thought 'e must be dying, at the very least, and there 'e is, with just a knocked shoulder.

'Can you keep this mobile canine thing orf me slippers, somebody? I don't want to 'ave to give it a kick.'

'Would you like to get back home now, Mummy McMurrough?' asked Bailey, and she nodded.

'I'll just get me shoes on and collect me 'andbag, and I'll be orf.' To Falconer, she added, 'Always wanted to be rich and famous when 'e were a kiddy, 'e did. Well, 'e's got it now, much good it's doing 'im. I've always said that you should be careful what you ask for, because you just might get it.'

'Does Mr McMurrough have any brothers or sisters?' asked the inspector, wondering if there could be any sibling rivalry behind these two recent mishaps.

''E's got three, but they're blood strangers now. They don't approve of 'im making a public spectacle of 'isself.'

'If you don't mind me saying so, Mrs McMurrough, you don't sound as if you come from the same place as your son; your accents are so dissimilar.'

'I should 'ope so, too. ''E were always tryin' to talk posh, from when 'e were a kid. Traitor to 'is roots, 'e is, but do you 'ear me complainin'? No, you don't. I've always told 'im to be 'oo 'e feels 'e is, and tell the rest of the world to go 'ang, and that's exac'ly what 'e's done. Can't say fairer than that, can yer?'

'Your attitude says much for your magnanimity,' replied Falconer, just before a plaintive voice spoke from the sofa.

'I *am* in the room, you know. And I *don't* appreciate being talked about in front of me like that.' McMurrough was missing the limelight. 'If you wish to dissect my character, kindly do it behind my back.'

And it was definitely going to be much too late to go to the pub tonight.

As Radcliffe ushered Mummy McMurrough out to the car, Falconer introduced Heather, and let her have a little gush in front of him, before he began his questioning.

When the two of them left half an hour later, Falconer promising to get someone out to collect the 'weapon', and any forensic evidence there may be, he said to Heather, 'Shall we go back to mine for a coffee? It's still quite early.'

'Great idea,' she replied. 'And there's something I need to ask you.' Leaving that threat hanging like a sword of Damocles, she enquired whether he'd like her to come over and cook Sunday roast for him, if both of them were off duty. It was quite a forward suggestion from her, as the invitation for coffee had overstepped bounds already set, and it would be her first visit to his home.

Having agreed in a somewhat nervous state, to this unexpected and unprecedented offer, the inspector spent the rest of the short drive back to Market Darley telling her about the traditional Sunday meal during his childhood years.

He had noticed, through the window of Glass House, a large floral centrepiece in the middle of the dining table. There had been no centrepiece in his home. Cook had always brought the lump of charred flesh to the table, and set it before his father with a defiant glare, which was returned in silent venom.

Every Sunday morning, his father would remind Cook that all of them like their meat pink, with the exception of chicken. Every Sunday lunchtime, he waged war on the tough, stringy lumps of charred meat, with which his ever-hopeful carving knife was presented.

The exception was, of course, the rare treat (in those days) of a chicken, which oozed dark pink juices as soon as he pierced its skin. Falconer Senior felt true hatred for the cook, who remained his *bête noir*, until he finally sacked her after a memorable Sunday when he had become incandescent with rage at the dry, solid, dark lump that sat, seemingly mocking him, from the carving plate.

He finally lost his grip on his temper, and wrestled the blasted lump off the plate, across the table and, eventually, to the floor, at which point Mrs Falconer had rung for Cook, requested that she open a tin of corned beef, then pack her bags forthwith, and leave the premises on a permanent basis.

Thereafter, the carving was always carried out in the kitchen, with silent savagery and frustration, by the matriarch of the family.

Heather laughed gleefully at the visions of this in her mind's eye, and declared that Sundays were never so dramatic in her childhood home, and suggested that this was probably because they couldn't afford to pay the wages of a cook.

While Falconer escorted his lady friend into his house, Chadwick McMurrough and Bailey Radcliffe in Fairmile Green settled down to watch McMurrough's chat show that they had recorded to watch at their leisure, Dipsy Daxie curled up, fast asleep, on his new master's lap, while Bailey leaned across and played lazily with the puppy's ears.

Back in Market Darley, the sense of tension began to grow in Falconer as Heather entered his home, and their coffee together became quite a stiff affair. He had few visitors, and the entrance of someone with whom he met regularly for social reasons bothered him more greatly than he had anticipated.

When he went to bed that night, it was with a real sense of foreboding and doom.

Chapter Three

Thursday
Market Darley

Harry Falconer could not believe his eyes. There was an open newspaper and a magazine left carelessly on the floor. On the coffee table were two almost empty cups, both stained with lipstick. Someone had disturbed his collection of ornaments, and they now sat out of place and muddled up. In the kitchen sink sat several pieces of crockery awaiting washing and, in the downstairs cloakroom, three pairs of ladies' tights hung on the radiator to dry.

'No! No! No!' he cried in revulsion and despair, and the cries woke him from this distressing nightmare. He lay for a while, his eyes bulging and staring at the ceiling, his fists clenched, sweat pouring from his body. His reaction to the very thought of someone sharing his house had produced a panic attack. The dream had been one of his rare, vivid ones, in colour.

Heather had asked him the previous evening if she could possibly stay – as in, move in – with him for a while. She had a limited time in the nurses' home, and it was nearly up, and although she had found a flat she wanted and made an offer on it, the legalities were not yet complete. It would only be for a few weeks, and they got on so well together.

He had sat on the fence, and said he would consider the idea. This nightmare had convinced him that the reality of the situation would rob him of his sanity. He had not realised how much he prized his personal space. His home was the den and he was the lion. There was no room in it for a lioness.

He was next rent with conflicting emotions: glad that his dream had polarised his opinion of sharing his home, albeit temporarily, and at the same time, filled him with trepidation that his refusal would jeopardise his friendship with Heather, but he couldn't think of a middle path.

The only thing he could think of doing was talking the situation over with Carmichael. He was much better at people than he was, and maybe he could suggest an acceptable solution to his awful dilemma. He could hardly explain to Heather that the thought of sharing his home made him feel physically sick. She had only spent half an hour in it the evening before, and his reaction had been extreme.

Falconer poured out his woes to his sergeant later that morning in a rather embarrassed manner. He was not proud of how he felt, and wondered if he was abnormal, but Carmichael soon put his fears to rest.

'A lot of people don't like sharing their home. When you look at your life so far, you had to sleep in a dormitory at school, then you shared a room when you were at university. I suppose you didn't have any private space when you first went into the army. It's no wonder that you value having somewhere that's just yours. It's something you haven't had a lot of, and it's become very important to you. That's nothing to be ashamed of. Don't beat yourself up about it. This country is full of people who live alone and, for a lot of them, it's by choice, not necessity; they're just very private people, like you. I'll tell you what, sir, we've got a spare room, and she's welcome to that, if she doesn't mind bunking in with a fairly chaotic family.'

'You couldn't do that,' protested Falconer. 'Whatever would Kerry say?'

'Kerry wouldn't mind at all. She got on with Heather fine when I was in hospital and, when's she's not on duty during the day, it'll be company for Kerry. I'll give her a ring if you like, and see how she feels about the idea. We'll think up some excuse for you to use to Heather, and everything will be all right again.'

'Carmichael, how can I thank you?'

'By coming over for lunch on Sunday.'

Carmichael didn't know it, but he was a double saviour. Now Falconer could politely decline Heather's offer to come over and cook for him on this particular occasion. He hadn't given her a definite answer, and he could now claim that he had a prior arrangement with his sergeant that he had temporarily forgotten.

It would be far less disturbing to spend the day with the family of five and their dogs, than to have someone other than himself working in his kitchen, cooking in his oven, and rummaging in his cupboards.

'Thank you so much. I should be delighted, Carmichael. What time would you like me to arrive?'

The inspector made a point of relaying this (fictitious) muddle-up in his social arrangements before Carmichael had the chance to talk to her, making the call as brief as possible so that she couldn't ask him whether he'd made a decision or not yet about her moving in with him – albeit temporarily.

Fairmile Green

In Glass House, tempers were rather frayed, as Dipsy had howled for much of the night, missing the mother and siblings to which he was used to curling up to sleep. The peacocks had also been unusually noisy, and no soul in the household was well rested.

Bailey had snapped at Chadwick when they first woke, and had stumped off downstairs to put some coffee on to brew, in the hope that he might feel a little more human, with some caffeine coursing through his veins.

Chadwick went into his en-suite – they each had their own, off different sides of the bedroom – for a shave, as he had not bothered the day before. As he plugged in his top of the range (of course!) razor, there was a bang and a flash, and he suddenly found himself on his bum, sprawled in the shower cubicle – definitely not amongst his short-term plans.

The short-circuit would normally have been enough to trigger the main circuit-breaker in the domestic distribution unit in the hall but, in this case, it had not. Although Bailey had been conscious of the noise, it did not trigger the fact that there was something wrong. The first intimation he had that there was something amiss had been a faint bleating noise of distress from upstairs.

Cold-heartedly staying to pour the water into the cafetière first, sure that there was nothing seriously out of kilter, he then slowly mounted the staircase, in the sure and certain knowledge that he would find Chadwick whingeing on about something really trivial, as usual.

Imagine his jolt of guilt, then, when he found his partner had suffered a serious electric shock that, had water been involved, could possibly have killed him. He helped the trembling Chadwick back to the bed, pulled the duvet over him, and marched downstairs to check the domestic distribution panel in the neat cupboard in the hall.

He could not believe his eyes when he saw that the circuit-breaker that should have been triggered by whatever the fault was, was actually taped in a way that prevented it from switching off the supply of electrical current. This was sabotage of the first order, and must have occurred when the trip-wire was affixed to the stairs, as there had been no other opportunity for someone with any sort of grudge to do so since then.

Bailey marched to the telephone in the hall and called Falconer's mobile number. This was getting really serious. It was not just a series of practical jokes or mild attempts to hurt Chadwick; this was attempted murder.

After venting his ire on the inspector, he went back upstairs with a cup of coffee for the invalid, only to be told, in the most scathing tones, that Chadwick would be grateful if he, Bailey, would mind removing his ratty old dressing gown from his, Chadwick's, bathroom, as it was cluttering up the place and making it look like a slum.

'You ungrateful bitch!' snapped Bailey. 'I should throw this coffee at you rather than just hand you the cup. I apologise for leaving it there. It was a rare aberration on my part, and I assure you it won't happen again.

'Trivialities aside, how are you feeling? I've checked the fuse box, and someone has actually taped down the circuit breaker. You could have been killed.'

'I feel ever so shaken,' moaned the invalid, placing the palm of one hand – the one not in possession of a cup of coffee – against his forehead in a most theatrical way.

'I'm not surprised. I've spoken to that police inspector again, and he and his sergeant are on their way over. I just hope that there aren't any more deadly traps lying in wait for you.'

'Oh, Gawd!' groaned Chadwick, with a quick return to the accent of his roots. 'So do I. I'm going to have to be ever so careful. Do you think I could get police protection?'

'We'll ask the nice inspector when he arrives. The

situation isn't much of a joke after this latest episode. Someone seems to have got it in for you, my little poppet.'

'In spades, ducky.'

'Drink your coffee before it gets cold.'

'Yes, Nanny.'

Market Darley

Harry Falconer answered the urgent summons of the telephone to find a furious Bailey Radcliffe on the end, with a tale of someone trying to electrocute his partner.

His tale was convincing enough to send a shiver of apprehension up the inspector's spine, as he realised someone didn't seem to be merely playing games with the new celebrity resident of the village, and if they were, they were playing for keeps. They really meant business, and meant to kill him, not merely inconvenience him with some minor injuries.

Ending the call, he grabbed his car keys from his jacket pocket, and hailed Carmichael. 'Come along with you. There's been a more serious attempt on Chadwick McMurrough's life. There was also an incident yesterday evening that I haven't had time to bring you up to date on yet. We need to go back to Fairmile Green. I'll tell you about last night on the way.'

Carmichael picked up his sunglasses and followed the inspector out of the office, his appetite whetted with the promise of details of an incident of which he had been, up to now, unaware, and the chance to see the star – his current personal hero – again.

Fairmile Green

Although the newcomers did not know it, there was

already a fair amount of resentment felt towards the new occupants of Glass House, some personal, from their past, and some more recent, to do with their refurbishment and occupation of that particular property, not to mention the installation of the peacocks.

While Chadwick McMurrough was recovering from the shock of his shock, there were many residents of the village who sat in their homes and fumed, on this bright and sunny day.

In the house to the left of Glass House as one looked down the village, Riverbanks, Gerald and Lucille Sutherland sat over a post-breakfast cup of coffee, bags under their eyes, their mouths constantly stretched by yawns.

'Those bloody birds!' exclaimed Gerald, once he could close his mouth with any degree of certainty that it would stay that way long enough for him to speak. 'I hardly got a wink of sleep last night. Apart from nightingales, I thought all birds were supposed to be quiet during the hours of darkness.'

'And that blasted dog,' chipped in Lucille. 'Did you hear that thing howling its head off half the night, as well?'

'It can't be allowed to go on. I know the animal's got to settle in, but those birds will have to go.'

'But what can we do?' asked Lucille, always first to the nub of the matter.

'When we've finished this coffee and I've woken myself up with a shower, I'll go out into the village with a clipboard and see if I can get up a petition, and we can then face our new neighbours with the local opposition.'

'Excellent idea! And while you're in the shower, I'll get the petition written and printed up on the computer.'

With a pained and put-upon expression, her husband added, 'After all that time when we had to put up with the work being done on the place, you'd think we'd have earned a bit of peace and quiet.'

Gerald had retired just as the refurbishment work had started on The Orchards to transform it into Glass House, and he thought he would go mad with the constant banging and noise from the various power tools. Then, just when the new owners had moved in and he thought things would settle down, the peacocks had been delivered and made their presence known in a very in-your-face, or perhaps in-your-earholes, way. Life seemed, sometimes, to be so unfair.

In self-defence, when the weather had improved, and the months wore on and the work still continued, he took to tucking his newspaper under his arm and heading, after breakfast on weekdays, to either Old Swan Yard or Darley Old Yard at the back of the shops in the High Street, where there were benches, and he could not hear the banging, hammering, and drilling quite so clearly.

On particularly bad days, he even went as far as Bear Pit Yard at the back of the parade of shops in Market Street, but he was sorely tried by having to evacuate his home directly after his retirement, because of noisy building work. To then be subjected, very shortly afterwards, by the constant shrill cries of God knew how many peacocks, to which mix was now added the howls of distress of a recently arrived puppy, was almost beyond both tolerance and belief.

After the night they had just endured, he was just in the right mood for toting a petition around the main streets and retail establishments of the village. He didn't know whether he'd gather enough signatures in one day, but he didn't mind that. He'd go out for as long as was necessary to get a goodly list of others who felt the even tenor of their lives was being disturbed by the current occupants of what he still thought of as The Orchards.

At least the builders had gone home in the evenings and

43

didn't work weekends. The animal part of this problem was what, although he hated to use the hackneyed expression, was called a twenty-four/seven one.

Two doors away, in Fairview, Keith and Kim Trussler were also in a similar mutinous mood. They both had jobs that required long hours and a fair amount of stress, and had previously treasured their evenings and weekends, weather permitting, either working or sitting in their garden. Now, both activities had become a nightmare, and had been so for several months.

They were similarly dismayed that the noise nuisance had not ceased when the last workman's truck had driven away, and a quick peek over the wall that separated their plot from the extensive rear garden of Glass House had revealed the presence of what looked like an industrial-sized barbecue and an enormous Jacuzzi.

Great! They inevitably indicated that there would be outdoor parties this summer, thus adding to the already disturbing and carrying cries for 'help' from the peacocks. They had chosen to buy their present home because of its quiet location, but with easy access to the local shops and to other towns and villages. Now, they felt that their peaceful private life had been wrested from their grasp, and that life had, somehow, cheated them; promising them paradise, only to deliver purgatory.

'But you've got to let them settle in, Keith. It's hardly fair that you go round and harangue them when the birds will probably get used to their surroundings and quieten down in the near future,' Kim pleaded with her husband, who had a very fiery temper when roused.

'Yes, and by then the parties will have started, all spilling out into the garden so that they can barbecue their food and frolic in that blasted Jacuzzi. I will not be driven to the expense and the sheer inconvenience of moving, just because we have neighbours who don't spare a thought for the others who live in close proximity to them. And they'll probably have parties that go on all night, because *they* don't have to get up in the mornings to go to a proper job.'

'A least give them a chance, Keith. There's nothing worse than being at war with the neighbours. It all gets so petty and spiteful, and nothing is ever solved, before someone has to move away, eventually, to put an end to it.'

'They've got a week,' declared her husband, with feeling, 'Then I'm going round to say my piece and, if that doesn't work, I'll contact the local authority's Noise Abatement Officer and get him to sort it out. Deal?'

'Deal.'

In Myrtle Cottage, on the other side of Glass House, Christopher and Christine Warren were trying to deal with their fractious and tired mob of four children, which consisted of Darren (six years old), Sharon (four), Karen (two), and Aron (six months).

None of the aforementioned had enjoyed an unbroken night's sleep, and it wasn't for the first time that this had happened. Neither were the youngest two able to indulge in their habitual afternoon nap any more. The new pets at The Orchards had seen to that.

It being the summer holidays, Christine had to spend her days with four young children, two of whom usually went to school and one to a playgroup, being quite advanced for her age. She was feeling hard done by, as it was still only the end of July, and she had nearly five weeks still to endure the current situation.

'You're going to have to go round there and say something, Chris,' she declared, a war-like glint in her eye.

'Not just yet. Give them a chance, Chris, love,' replied her husband, not eager for combat and in the hope that,

45

given a couple more days, everything would be back to normal.

'But it's not fair. You get to go into the office every day where it's quiet and peaceful. I'm stuck here with those filthy birds screaming their heads off, that dog of theirs howling and barking, and four whingeing kids to put the tin lid on the situation.' The war-like glint had turned to an expression of self-pity, and her eyes welled up with tears at her plight. 'Please don't go into the office today. Stay here and help me cope.'

'You know I can't do that. And what good would it do? If I were here instead of at work, it wouldn't shut the birds or the dog up. OK, I could take the kids off your hands for a couple of hours, but that would be about it; and you know we've got a rush on at the moment. With jobs as rare as they are at the moment, I daren't risk mine by taking time off for trivial reasons.'

'Trivial?' his wife queried, and burst into tears.

Others in the village had more personal reasons for resentment. Dean Westbrook lived in a tiny cottage in Old Darley Passage, a minute access road that led down to Darley Old Yard, in a property labelled 2B.

When he had first heard it rumoured that Chadwick McMurrough had bought The Orchards, and was going to spend a fortune on doing it up, Dean had begun to shake uncontrollably. When McMurrough had actually moved in, he decided that he would have to stop using the village pub and shops in case he bumped in to him.

The reason for this mood of rank terror in meeting the man was because McMurrough had bullied Dean Westbrook mercilessly through years of their shared schooling. The very thought of the latest media darling made Dean feel physically sick, and he was seriously considering turning his very satisfactory life upside-down

46

by moving somewhere else, where there was no risk of seeing his one-time tormentor; the evil psyche that had been the ruination of his childhood. His antipathy and fear of Chadwick was so strong that, occasionally, recently, he had wondered if it may be advisable for him to seek some psychiatric help.

Only his mother was aware of how he felt, and she had offered him a place to stay, temporarily, back at home, if he needed somewhere while he sought alternative accommodation. But, why should he be the one to move? Why should he have his life turned inside-out by something that happened – granted, over a very long period – years ago, before he achieved adulthood. It was cowardly even to consider this drastic course of action.

In the adjoining, similarly bijou cottage, labelled 'Or Not 2B', lived Gareth Jones. It had been he who was responsible in the first place for McMurrough being aware of Fairmile Green, and the fact that The Orchards was up for sale at a knock-down price because of the river running underneath it – it being, therefore, unmortgageable, and needing a cash buyer – and the amount of updating it would need to make it habitable.

Gareth Jones was, in fact, Chadwick McMurrough's ex-partner, whom McMurrough had dumped pretty swiftly after meeting Bailey when he was working on *Cockneys*.

A television director beat an electrician hands down, in Chadwick's eyes, and he felt no loyalty whatsoever to the man for whom he had once declared his undying love. Unfortunately for Gareth Jones, the stars in McMurrough's eyes had obscured his vision, and his love had caught a bad case of Asian Flu, and succumbed immediately unto death.

Jones was left alone and lonely, feeling that he had been rooked out of his share of the limelight, where he could have basked in the spotlight of his partner's success. Now, instead of being the long-term partner of a famous media person, he was just 'Gareth Jones, Electrician, No job too small', as it said on his business card.

It should have been him, living down in the big house in the lap of luxury, instead of stuck back here in this poky little hole, with no one to share his time with. Life had definitely dealt him a bum hand.

Bailey Radcliffe, too, had had a long-term partner when he had met Chadwick McMurrough on the set of *Cockneys*. They had even bought a property together, but as soon as Bailey announced his intention of leaving for the love of another, the house went on the market, and sold unbelievably quickly.

His partner had been Darren Worsley, who had taken his share of the money and rented a tatty old house for peanuts, coincidentally, also in Old Darley Passage, opposite the pair of semi-detached cottages. His share of the house money he had rapidly disposed of in pubs, clubs, and off-licences, drowning his sorrows at losing not only his partner, but his home and rosy future too.

Bailey had been the older and more stable partner in this relationship, as he was in his current one, and Darren had reverted back to the loser he had been when he had first met Radcliffe and been encouraged to get his act together. Now, he was a wreck of a young man again but, this time, with no one to pick him up and set him on his feet again.

He could not believe his bad luck in moving to the very village where his ex-partner and his new young partner were to make their home. He, similarly, dreaded running into either one of them in the street, but for a different reason. He was afraid he would not be able to control his rage at the sight of either one of the pair that he thought had stolen his life and his stable future.

He'd already lost his job through his frequent drink-fuelled absences; not that it had been much of a job, as Bailey had earned such a good wage. On his own, he'd never have been able to pay the mortgage on the property they had bought together, let alone buy out his ex-partner's share.

He was definitely the loser, and there should be some way he could get recompense. He was sitting, oblivious of the gorgeous day outside, brooding on just this problem.

Chapter Four

Thursday
Fairmile Green

When Falconer and Carmichael arrived at Glass House, it was Bailey Radcliffe who answered the door to their summons. Chadwick McMurrough was still upstairs, getting dressed for the visit of the policemen.

When Bailey had gone up to the bedroom about half an hour ago, Chadwick had been discovered still lying, now on top of the duvet, with his hands one on each side of his head.

'Whatever's up with you, ducky?' asked Bailey.

'It's those blasted birds yelling. I've got such a headache. I wonder if you could be a sweetie and get me some painkillers from my bathroom.'

'I'd better get some from mine. Yours is probably off limits until there's been a forensic team over it.'

'Good thinking, Bails. Do you think you could go downstairs after I've taken my medication and tape up their bloody beaks? I feel like I'll never experience silence again.'

'That's what you get for being so precipitate, without thinking things through first. Remember that old Spanish proverb: Take what you want, says God, And pay for it. Well, you're paying for it now. As are the neighbours, I hasten to add. I'm surprised we haven't had hordes of people round banging on the door to complain.'

'Give them time,' replied Chadwick with a wince. 'Whatever am I going to do about it?'

'Put them on eBay.'

'The neighbours?'

'The peacocks, silly.'

'Where on earth would I advertise? What section? Large group of peacocks for sale: knockdown price. Owner collects. Do they have a section for upper-crust things like that?'

'The abattoir?' retorted his partner, with an evil grin. 'I suggest, however,' continued Bailey, in more measured tones, 'that I phone the local vet and ask if he knows of any local animal sanctuary that would take them at short notice. That will give you a chance to phone whoever – the maniacs – supplied the things in the first place and see if they'll take them back, even if that means accepting a credit note, as long as you don't use it to acquire a nice boa constrictor. We'll take it from there, depending on what they have to say.'

'The voice of reason, as usual,' commented Chadwick, with a sigh of relief that his ordeal may be about to come to an end. 'Anyway, that's enough about those damned birds. Now, back to me.'

'There's the doorbell. That'll be the police. Get yourself looking respectable and come down, so they can question you.'

Downstairs, the three men had just taken seats in the living room when Chadwick joined them, looking none the worse for his ordeal and his headache. 'Sorry about all this to-ing and fro-ing. I really do seem to be in somebody's bad books with all these attacks. I just can't think whose,' Chadwick greeted them.

'It's better to be safe than sorry, sir,' replied Falconer.

'Their next attempt might be more successful, therefore it's vital that we find out who is responsible for these incidents before you are seriously hurt, or worse.'

'We've arranged for someone from SOCO to come over and go through your bathroom for any evidence that might help in identifying the perpetrator,' interjected Carmichael, who still had stars in his eyes.

'Don't forget the domestic distribution unit – what we in the old days used to call the fuse box. He'll have been in there to stick down the circuit-breaker,' added Bailey.

'Good thinking, sir. Now, Mr McMurrough, if you wouldn't mind telling me, in your own words, exactly what happened when you went into your bathroom this morning?'

When everything that could be told had been told, Bailey saw the detectives out of the house, while Chadwick again put a hand theatrically across his forehead to indicate suffering.

As soon as his partner re-entered the room, he perked up miraculously, and said, 'I say, Bails, it's a gorgeous day, for once. The summer's been foul and wet so far. Let's take advantage of it and have a barbecue party this evening.'

'But we don't know anyone yet,' retorted Bailey, a frown briefly distorting his features.

'Liar, liar, pants on fire!' replied his partner childishly, in a sing-song voice. 'We know Gareth, my ex, in the little place down the Passage. And if we printed off invitations on the computer, we could put them through all the neighbours' doors, and get to meet them that way – all at once, as it were – get the whole thing over with.'

'You clever boy. Then, if anyone's got any gripes with us, they can all complain at once, and we won't be plagued with people for ever knocking on the door to give us grief. And, if I phone the vet fairly sharpish, we'll be able to tell them that arrangements are already in hand to solve the immediate noise-nuisance problem.'

'I'll work one up on the computer right away and, when I've printed off the copies, you can take them round and shove them through letterboxes,' suggested Chadwick, with a smirk.

'I know why you're looking at me like that. If anyone opens the door while I'm shoving the invitation through, it'll be me that gets all the grief.'

When he went out on his delivery errand, half an hour later, he commented, before he closed the door, that there was someone in the main street with a clipboard stopping people, as if he had a petition. 'I haven't got time to see what it's about now, as we've got to get ready for this party If he's still there tomorrow I'll go and see what he's up to,' Bailey shouted through to Chadwick, before slamming the door shut.

'Aren't you the clever one, then?' McMurrough got up and went over to the work station where they kept their downstairs computer. Time to check fan messages on his Facebook page, and get his ego stroked. That always put him in a good mood.

If the Good Language Fairy had been listening to what was being said in Fairmile Green later that day, she'd have been absolutely scandalised at the comments made when the residents discovered they had been invited to a party at *that* house.

'Bloody cheek!'

'The sheer damned brass neck of it!'

'How dare they?'

'How thick-skinned can you get?'

'Well, I'm sodding well going just to have my say about their bloody birds.'

Yes, the poor GLF had a definite need for earplugs by the evening of that day.

Castle Farthing

When Carmichael got home that night, quite tired now that he was going into work regularly and getting up rather earlier than he had been used to of late, he immediately asked Kerry about having Heather to stay for a few weeks.

'It won't be for a long time, and you know what the boss is like about his things; his home; everything being just so? I don't know how he's going to explain it to her, but he'd better be very inventive, or she'll take umbrage and think he simply doesn't want her around any more.'

'How very perceptive of you, Davey,' replied his wife. 'And, of course, she can come to stay. As you said, it won't be for ever, she'll be company for me when you're at the station, and she'll be a distraction for the kids. It doesn't matter that there's plenty of us here already – bring it on, I say.'

As she finished speaking, there was a knock at the front door, and her husband went to answer it as Kerry was just about to serve up their evening meal.

On the doorstep he found Mr and Mrs Moore from further down the row of cottages, with their Great Dane, Mulligan. This enormous creature had stayed with the Carmichaels on a few occasions in the past – one memorable time being the previous Christmas, when Falconer had also, by default, had to stay as well.

'Hello, you three. How can I help you?' Carmichael asked politely.

'We wouldn't ask if we weren't desperate,' began Mr Moore, with a worried expression.

'It's the kennels, you see,' interrupted his wife. 'They

simply won't, any more.'

'Won't what?'

Mulligan, not understanding anything of the conversation could, however, scent the children, the resident two little dogs, and one of the favourite places in his small canine world. He started with a fairly desperate whine then, when none of the people present took any notice of him, did what he always did when he wanted something and no one seemed about to oblige.

Pulling on his lead and, due to his superior weight and strength, dragging Mr Moore, perforce, with him, he entered the house, with his hapless master being dragged unwillingly behind him, trailed along haplessly like the tail of a kite. 'Hold on, Mulligan, boy. We haven't been asked in,' pleaded Mr Moore with an apologetic grin, his head turned almost backwards towards Carmichael.

'Let's just stop and go back outside, there's a good doggy,' Moore cajoled, without hope in his voice. He was going to lose this tussle, as he always did all the other differences of opinion he had with his pet.

'Hello there, Mulligan. Would you like a nice biscuit?' Kerry's voice sounded, so the huge creature had evidently reached the kitchen.

'Hello, Mrs Carmichael. Sorry about this, but I think Mulligan just wanted to say hello,' the hapless owner excused himself.

'No problem, Mr Moore. Mulligan's always welcome here. You know that,' she replied, her last words almost drowned out by two whoops of childish delight and, some excited high-pitched yapping.

'I think the rest of the family has just realised we've got a visitor. Don't worry about it, Mrs Moore,' said Carmichael with a smile.

'But, from the smells, I assume you're just about to eat.'

'No problem. We always have dog food in this house, and I don't see any reason why we can't rustle up a bowl of something tasty for one of our favourite animals. You leave him here to play for a while, and I'll bring him back when the children go to bed – see if we can't tire him out a bit for you.'

'That's so kind of you,' Mrs Moore replied, and called her husband back out to the door.

'Now, what's this problem you've got with the kennels?'

'They won't have Mulligan,' she told him. 'We're going on holiday early on Monday morning, and we'd booked him in for a fortnight. Then, this morning, they phoned and the owner said they wouldn't be able to take him any more, because his wife is terrified of him, and he's such a big softie, really – Mulligan, that is, not the owner of the kennels.

'And you know our daughter can't have him – we told you all about that last Christmas, when you so kindly stepped into the breach – and we don't want to have to cancel our holiday. We do so like the Algarve, too,' Mrs Moore added, pleadingly.

As if to emphasise the urgency of the request, Mulligan whined pathetically, and offered his paw to Carmichael, as if in entreaty.

'Don't give it another thought,' Carmichael replied with a broad grin, accepting the paw and shaking it solemnly. 'We love having him here. Just bring him and his bits and pieces on Sunday, then you can get your packing done in peace.'

'Oh, you are a darling!'

'You're a diamond,' said Mr Moore. 'I don't care what other people say about the police. I think you're great.'

'Thank you,' replied Carmichael, slightly puzzled by this dubious compliment. 'Bring him along on Sunday, and you can pick him up when you're back and unpacked.'

Going back into the kitchen, he apprised Kerry of their extra lodger, this one four-legged. 'I do love Mulligan,' she said, then added in a voice with more urgency in it, 'I know you'll have to get in a big supply of dog food and biscuits, but could you do it tomorrow and, while you're about it, pick me up another gas bottle – maybe on the way home from work? I've got a couple of days left in this one, probably, but I don't like to run too short.'

'Will do,' replied her husband, making a mental note to do as his wife requested. She didn't often ask anything of him, and it was the least he could do to respond promptly to the few requests she made, and this last one was of prime importance, out where they lived.

Although people in nearby towns who had no friends or relatives out in the sticks would hardly credit it, mains gas did not, as yet, reach as far as the villages, and they had to survive with bottled gas for both hobs, and fires, the latter whether static or mobile.

Market Darley

Harry Falconer also had not long arrived home – to a blessedly empty house – and had made himself a good, strong cup of tea, had a bit of a sit and a ponder, and now proposed to phone Heather with his explanation for why he could not put her up. He sat with fingers crossed, hoping for similar luck to that which he had had for her acceptance of his muddle-up for a roast meal this Sunday.

He had not long ago received a call from Carmichael telling him that everything was hunky-dory for her to stay with them, and he thought he had his story finely tuned, now, for credibility.

Falconer: Hello, Heather? Harry here.

Heather: Hello there. To what do I owe this pleasure?

Falconer: It's about you having to leave the nurses' home, and needing somewhere interim to stay while you wait for the legalities on your flat sale and purchase to be completed.

Heather: Is this call to tell me I *can* move into yours?

Falconer: Not exactly. I've made arrangements for you to stay with my sergeant, Davey Carmichael. He's married with children, but his home is two cottages knocked into one, so there's plenty of room.

Heather: Oh! (surprised). That's very kind of them, but why? I thought I could just stay with you.

Falconer: There are unforeseen problems with me having people to stay.

Heather: And they are what? (huffily).

Falconer: I've never explained to you fully about my cats.

Heather: Your cats? What's so special about your cats that they stop me staying with you?

Falconer: There are five of them, and three of them used to belong to murderers. My original cat is still getting used to not being an 'only', and the last one to arrive – well, we don't know anything about her past at all. I've not had four of them terribly long and know virtually nothing about what they endured before they moved in with me, but I do know that they're very easily upset. His crossed fingers were now for the lies he was telling, rather than for good luck.

I am their stable home now, and I don't want them to be unsettled and feel they can't come into the house because someone new and unknown has supplanted them. I know how sensitive you are to feelings (in a wheedling voice) and I felt that, of all the people in my acquaintance, – (don't slip into pomposity just when victory is in sight) – you would understand.

Heather: I think you're mad, but I sort of see where

58

you're coming from.

Falconer: I'm very sorry about the situation, but I don't really have any choice. If anyone comes in, they disappear out of the cat flap, and don't come back again until they know the coast is clear. If you moved in, heaven alone knew when I'd see them again.

Heather: I believe you; thousands wouldn't.

Falconer: I'll give you a ring about our next meal, OK?

Heather: Agreed. Bye. I'll wait to hear from you then, and you can give me the number for where I'll be staying.

Falconer: I'll do that now, then you'll have everything you need.

He was being as cagey as possible. After his chilling dream of the previous night, he was well and truly spooked. He had neither made a firm arrangement with her for their next meal, nor asked her if she'd like to make coming in for coffee a regular part of their outings.

Fairmile Green

Bailey Radcliffe had had a quick latte, then got straight into the car and driven to Market Darley to raid the shelves of its supermarkets, so that they had sufficient food and drink to serve their guests that evening.

His mind was awash with items that he needed to purchase: red wine, white wine, gin, tonic water, whisky, beer; that would do for drinks, with some squashes and juice. Now for food: pork chops, lamb chops – very pricey – sausages, burgers, rolls, bags of salad, baking potatoes. Better get some veggie burgers and sausages as well, in case there were any food freaks amongst their neighbours.

Oh, and he mustn't forget nibbles for while people were waiting for food to cook. This was going to cost a fortune. Lucky that Chadwick was paying, then – it was his idea, so he was responsible for any expenses incurred.

Meanwhile, back at the house, Chadwick was busy putting together a couple of large lasagnes for anyone who wanted to eat before the food on the barbecue was ready. He was very conscious of people's differing tastes, so he very deliberately made sure that one of these dishes was vegetarian.

What he would not advertise was that he had 'accidentally' fried off the vegetables for this in lard, out of sheer badness. Michael Jackson hadn't patented the word, after all, and the lettuce munchers would never notice what he'd done if he didn't say anything about it.

Later, as they were dividing the meat (and vegetarian options) on and into metal trays ready to be cooked, while Dipsy got underfoot making little begging yips, Chadwick asked rather apprehensively, 'What if no one turns up? We haven't had any RSVPs. Oh, do get out of the way, Dipsy. It's no wonder I trod on you, if you will wander between my feet like that.'

'Did you put RSVP at the bottom of the invitations?'

'No.'

'Well, there you are then. I'll tell you what,' Bailey began in a soothing voice. 'If no one comes to our party, the food will keep until tomorrow, then you can ring the production team from *Chadwick's Chatterers*, and we'll make it a party for your show.'

'You're absolutely brilliant, my clever darling. Have you done anything about getting my character back into *Cockneys* yet?'

'Not yet, but I've planted a few seeds in a few minds, so that, when I do, it'll be almost as if it's their own idea.'

'You always were a cunning bastard. Look at the way you lured me from Gareth's arms.'

'That was nothing to the way you lured me away from

Darren's clutches, Chad.'

'Aren't we naughty, Bails?'

'Yes, but nice – decidedly *nice* boys, don't you think?'

'Oh, you are awful,' replied Chadwick, as he checked his lasagnes' progress in the oven. They were very nearly done. 'Oh, my God! Apart from the obvious, they'll all be straight, won't they?'

'Yep. Apart from the obvious, I expect we're the only two gays in the village.'

'Very funny.'

'By the way, I went along to the first house in Market Street with the invitations to our little soirée, and I put them into the doors of all three houses in Old Darley Yard, where your darling ex lives. It was the only way I could keep tabs on the guy with the petition. I've got the nasty feeling it was about us.'

'Just as well,' replied Chadwick drily, as it felt like 'back to me' time.

Elsewhere in the villages, local voices were raised, again, in anger.

'I'll not cross his threshold, the shallow little git.'

'I'll not change into my best for those two bleeding faggots.'

'Who the hell does he think he is, thinking he just has to whistle and I'll come to him?'

'I'll complain quietly, if you like, but I'm going to have my say, if it kills me.'

'Who do they think they are, summoning us as if we were the village peasants, in need of a square meal?'

'How he's got the nerve to think I'd want to socialise with the two of them, I simply don't know. Not after what happened.'

'Well they can bloody well put up with the kids for a couple of hours. I've had them all day, and I could do with a break. If their stuff's too precious for little hands, they'd damned well better keep the doors shut, hadn't they?'

It didn't matter what was said, however. Everyone who had received an invitation was hell-bent on seeing the inside of that house, now it had been gutted and had new owners, whatever their beef with them was.

The first guests arrived five minutes early at twenty-five past six. Fortunately, the party-throwers had finished their preparations just before six o'clock, with the lighting of the charcoal, so that it would be heated up by a reasonable time. They didn't want this to turn into a late night.

The early arrivals were, in fact, the gaggle that composed the Warren family from Myrtle Cottage. Both Christopher and Christine composed their lips into smiles as they were bidden enter, but their eyes were hostile, and had the glint of anger in them. With them came four children, one a babe in arms.

At sight of the open back wall, the three ambulatory small people set off for the garden at a run, and Bailey and Chadwick welcomed their parents more formally. This was, however, doomed not to be a long visit.

Bailey went to the open back wall to keep an eye on the children for safety reasons, as the barbecue was alight, and found them chasing the peacocks with great whoops of childish delight. 'Stop that immediately!' he called, and went outside to herd them back into the house, leaving the birds sulking, either in the shrubbery or their little wooden house, in fear.

Once inside, the children discovered Dipsy and, no sooner had Bailey procured their parents a drink, than he heard a roar of rage from Chadwick emanating from the kitchen. 'He's not a toy dog. He's real, and you'll really hurt him. How dare you try to poke him in the eyes!'

Before Radcliffe could make a move to leave the sitting room, three short forms hurtled into the room, all of them having burst into tears at being chided twice in a very short space of time. They simply didn't know the rules where peacocks and domestic pets were concerned, and felt that they should not be admonished if no one had explained things to them.

Bailey and Chadwick, similarly, didn't know the rules with children, and didn't realise how heavy-handed they could seem.

Christine immediately took umbrage on her offspring's behalf, thrust Aron into his father's arms (thus starting him off to grizzle) and put her arms around the other three. 'Did the nasty man shout at you, my darlings?' she cooed, a velvet maternal machine now, her whining about being stuck with them all day, before they had left home, now completely forgotten in her defence of them.

Knowing they were on to a good thing here, the three children sobbed even harder, until Christine stood up and said, 'Come along, Christopher. We're not staying here to see our children mistreated. Them and their bloody peacocks. We're going home. Now!'

On their indignant march down the path, they met one set of next-door neighbours, just about to enter by the gate. Noticing this new arrival, Bailey and Chadwick didn't even bother closing the door between visitors, but stood with it open, smiling brightly at the next arrivals, and hoping that their visit would be slightly longer and a bit more successful than the last one.

Once again, the mouths were smiling, but the eyes told a different story. This couple also looked as if it had a score to settle, but was willing to keep the lid on it for now. Inviting them in and supplying them with a drink each, they had no time to talk, as the doorbell rang again, and the Sutherlands – for this is who they had been – were succeeded by the Trusslers.

After that, a steady stream of people arrived. Invitations had been issued to eleven households in all and, although the Warrens had already exited in a huff, there were still plenty of guests to supply with drinks and tempt to nibbles. As they were all from the same village, they also knew each other, so conversation flowed in a very satisfactory way.

The only awkward moments were the arrivals of Gareth Jones and Darren Worsley. Even these two entered the throng with a fair grace, but as both had ulterior motives for being there, that was hardly surprising.

Bailey took himself out into the garden to barbecue the various offerings he had purchased earlier that day, and Chadwick took up duty in the kitchen by their supply of drinks. If anyone wanted to talk to either of them specifically – probably to complain about the birds or even, maybe, the workmen – both of them were easy enough to find.

Both of the hosts had noticed a significant difference between how the couples had dressed. It was obvious that the guests had a bone to pick with them, and this was no surprise, but the two sexes had dealt with registering their disapproval in how they dressed for their first visit to the newly refurbished property.

Mainly, the men had opted for a very casual look, showing their displeasure in tatty old jeans and washed-out T-shirts. The women, on the other hand, had dressed to the nines and, literally, put on the war paint, to go into battle.

Two of the men, namely Darren Worsley and Gareth Jones, having identified that they were the aggrieved parties at this gathering, had formed a small huddle in a quiet part of the garden and were having a grand bitch about who had suffered the most humiliation and potential loss of glittering future.

Representatives of the other neighbouring properties approached either Bailey or Chadwick individually, attempting to have an, in the main, civilised discussion about their distress at the disruption the various noise nuisances had caused in their households.

An eavesdrop around the various guests would have gleaned the following conversations.

On a bench, well away from the barbecue and Jacuzzi, Gareth Jones was putting his case for having lost the most, as far as future lifestyle was concerned. 'He was nothing, when he was with me. The only thing he did was put in an application form for that damned silly show.

'I told him he was wasting his time – what did I know? I thought he had a very slim chance of being chosen for it and, if he was, he would only be humiliated and ridiculed with the clever way they edit the film for however long he lasted.

'I had absolutely no idea that he might actually win, and suddenly be the flavour of the month. That part in *Cockneys* was just out of the blue, and the vain bugger did nothing but boast about how famous he was, and what a glittering future he had ahead of him.

'I told him not to take anything for granted, and I felt vindicated when he only had the part for a few weeks, but then along came the offer of the chat show, and all my warnings of caution were blown out of the water.

'And he'd got mixed up with one of the directors on *Cockneys*, so I was for the chop even when he was in that, although I didn't realise it at the time. I just thought his distraction was due to getting used to the change in his fortunes. I must admit, I thought things were about to look up, and was really looking forward not to having to watch where all the money went.

'Then, boom! I was dumped good and proper. Chad

just said he'd taken up with someone else who was "in the business", and it was all over. He said it never would have worked with us because of his new position, and I was merely his past – callous bastard.'

Darren Worsley now took up the baton, and ran with his side of this rectangular story. 'We always watched *The Glass House*, and I hate to admit it, but we were rooting for Chad McMurrough. It was inevitable, I suppose, with both us and him being gay.

'Looking back, I can see that Bailey was rather more interested in him as a contestant than was healthy, but I must admit, I thought nothing of it at the time. Then the slime-ball won, and the next thing I knew, Bailey started burbling about him having a short contract on *Cockneys*.

'That was what started me worrying. Bailey seemed to be lit up at the idea, which was not like him at all. He was normally such a calm person. Then he started having a lot of out of normal hours meetings, and I began to feel very uncomfortable.

'The next big event was him arriving home in a taxi, utterly off his face and clutching a half-empty bottle of champagne. That was the day that McMurrough signed the contract for his chat show, and they'd decided to give things a go together. Never mind about old loyalties: pleasure, now, seemed to be their motto.

'He dumped me in a very drunken manner that night, called another taxi, and sped off to some hotel to spend the night with his new love. I was in the past: gone, and probably forgotten, too. Why I got an invitation to this charade I have no idea. Maybe it's in place of an apology but, if that's the case, it's too little, too late, and I don't accept it. I hate him. And I'm going to drink his new palace dry tonight, if I can.'

'Just how I feel about Chad,' echoed Gareth gloomily into his glass. 'But that's not going to stop me going for a burger and a sausage. I might even take a few snaps with my phone, if an opportunity presents itself.'

'Get me something to eat, too, will you. After all, it's not your ex cooking the food, is it?' pleaded Darren, 'and I'll refresh the glasses.'

'And it's not you who's got a dossier on this despicable pair to leak to the press when the opportunity presents itself,' muttered Gareth. And he did, indeed, have a lot of dirt on the couple. His dossier included candid shots taken with a long lens since they had purchased their present home, shots of them outside the studio in each other's arms, and shots of Gareth with Chad before he had become famous; a lot of old stuff too from when they were a couple.

Hell hath no fury like a queen scorned, and Gareth was hoping to make a nice little packet out of what he had put together, in some ways as compensation for the lifestyle which he considered had been stolen from him by Bailey. But he'd have to pounce while Chad was still flavour of the month, in case he proved just to be a nine days' wonder.

Like so many other people who had emerged from reality shows as great celebrities, many found themselves, three months later, queuing back at the benefits office, back where they had come from, fame and fortune just a distant memory. He must do something positive with what he had while Chad was still hot property.

Darren wandered back into the house with a dim thought in his befuddled brain that maybe there was a way to get revenge. Maybe he could blackmail Bailey in some way. Or maybe there was another way to get his own back?

Chapter Five

Still at the party

Dean Westbrook was next in to the kitchen after Darren Worsley. It had taken him up to now to gather the necessary courage to confront his old bully. He was still a young man, and his schooldays didn't really seem that far off to him. It took a great deal of screwing himself up to actually enter the kitchen and confront Chadwick about his behaviour in the past.

'How's it going, Dean?' asked Chadwick, as the timid figure entered the room from the garden.

'I n-need to speak to you about s-something,' Dean stuttered nervously.

'Can't get you into "the business", dearie,' declared McMurrough. 'I don't have that kind of influence just yet. But give me time.'

'No, no, it was nothing like that. It was about when we were at school together?'

'Oh, do carry on. You intrigue me greatly.'

When Dean left the kitchen with his now full glass, he was as white as a sheet. He didn't remember. The shallow slime-ball had absolutely no recollection of his past unspeakable behaviour. That cruel scum simply didn't remember bullying him. In fact, he had no recall of picking on him whatsoever, and seemed to think that they had co-existed quite happily together in the same classroom. He was so angry that he took himself off to a quiet corner where he could seethe in peace, and collect his thoughts.

How could he have forgotten? How could he just not remember? It had caused him sleepless nights at the time: almost driven him to suicide, and haunted him ever since, and Chadwick McMurrough simply didn't remember. He had no conscience whatsoever about ruining a teenage boy's life, and he'd never even had the grace to feel sorry.

This simply wasn't good enough. When he thought of all the agony he had gone through at this bully's whims, he felt physically sick, and all McMurrough could say was that he didn't recall anything of that sort. Well, he'd have to pay now; now that he, himself, was stronger – an adult. He'd find a way to make the sadist pay for all those tears and all that fear he had suffered. And the nightmares: he'd pay for those, too. How bold alcohol makes us.

Christopher Warren re-appeared in the garden. After stalking off with the rest of his family, he had evidently decided to come back to make his real feelings felt in a little more detail, and used the side gate. Bailey saw his approach and made a mental note to get bolts for this handy entrance and exit, which was already proving more trouble than it was worth.

'Sorry to bother you,' apologised Warren. 'I've come back, really, on behalf of the wife. You know how they like to have their say – oh, I say, I am sorry, but of course you don't.'

He was starting to get a bit tongue-tied with embarrassment, and Bailey put him at his ease and bade him continue. If the man was going to make a complaint, he might as well get it over with as quickly as possible.

'It's not so much about during the day,' Chris Warren

began. 'I know I'm out at work and Christine's at home with the kids, and they do miss their afternoon naps, the younger ones, but, the main problem is in the evening and at night.

'We used to have a charmed existence – if such a thing exists – with how quiet life was in Fairmile Green. Then, you bought this place, and the workmen moved in.' Here, Warren tried an ingratiating smile that didn't quite come off.

'I mean, that wasn't too bad, because at least they went home after the working day, but now you've got these exotic birds, and I fear they're making our lives hell. I wouldn't bother if it was just me, I'd simply wear earplugs. Chris takes it so much harder, you see, what with the kids and everything.

'You can hardly put earplugs into a six-month-old baby's ears, now can you? Nor can you explain to him why he doesn't get enough peace and quiet to have a couple of hours' kip in the afternoons. And that applies to Karen, our two-year-old, as well. I'm sorry to come round complaining like this, but Chris – my wife – insisted that something be said on behalf of the whole family.'

Chadwick, who was not very fond of children, being the second of four, himself, was not very sympathetic, having wandered out from the kitchen to have a word with his partner. He had been quietly but steadily quaffing gin and tonic while he served others with drinks, and found that he was already rather sloshed.

Instead of the quiet courtesy that Bailey would have shown this neighbour, Chadwick sent him off with a flea in his ear about 'live and let live', and promising to get him some prospectuses for boarding schools to relieve his wife's burden of care. Had they not, as new residents, had to put up with the squalling of his tribe of brats on a daily basis? He was feeling really 'bad' this evening.

McMurrough, in a bit of a huff that after all their spending and preparation all he was going to reap from their party tonight were complaints, went through to the telephone and rang all the members of the *Chadwick's Chatterers* production crew and asked them to come round. If it was turning into war, then he needed troops for his side, to counteract those in the opposing army.

Then, deciding that their hostile guests were perfectly capable of working out how to pour their own drinks, he went back to the kitchen for another drink, grabbed his newly refilled glass, and stomped off out into the garden to join Bailey again. At least they were on the same side together.

As they stood together in solidarity at the barbecue, the side gate creaked again, and a woman came into view, her arms filled with the figure of Dipsy Daxie, her face a mask of fury.

'I suppose this is your damned dog,' she called from nearly the other side of the garden.

'His name's Dipsy,' called back Chadwick, with no idea what the problem was.

'I don't care if his name is Winston Churchill. He's evidently slipped through your security somehow – unless, of course, you let him run loose, which is most irresponsible – and he's got under my fencing and had it off with my Darling.'

This most confusing conclusion to her complaint gave both Chad and Bailey visions of Dipsy making eyes at the woman's husband. 'My Darling is a pedigree and she's in season, waiting for a visit from a stud to cover her tomorrow. Now your damned animated sausage has got in first, and God knows what the outcome will be.'

'But Dipsy's too young to do that sort of thing,' countered Chadwick in indignation.

'Oh no he's not, Mr High-and-Mighty. I've got footage of the very act itself, on my phone, if you want to see it.' She was nearly in front of them now, but had not moderated the volume of her voice at all.

'May I suggest that we converse a little more quietly madam, and that you introduce yourself. We're, naturally, very sorry if Dipsy has disgraced himself, but we had no idea that he could get out. We've only had him for a very short time, and the situation hasn't arisen before.'

It was lucky that Bailey had spoken, because Chadwick had had such a volume of gin that he would have been decidedly less polite, and probably told them to go hang, or worse.

'What breed is your dog, madam?' Bailey was back on the diplomatic road to a peace treaty.

'I'm Ellie Smallwood from Green Gates and darling Darling's a little Shih Tzu.'

'She must be, if she let my Dipsy raunch her, and them not even introduced properly.' Chadwick had spoken this unadvised opinion before Bailey could stop him, and the face of their female guest, which had been clearing of its thunder clouds, suddenly darkened again, as she dropped Dipsy without any ceremony whatsoever.

'If my sweetie, darling Darling gives birth to a litter of mongrel puppies, I'm going to sue the pants off both of you for canine assault and impregnation without permission,' Ellie Smallwood positively roared into Chadwick's face, and his became as storm cloud-ridden as hers.

Ellie gave him no chance to retort, but turned away immediately and headed for the side gate again, while Dipsy took advantage of the opportunity of proximity to his owner to cock his leg with fear. The woman had scared him, and he didn't feel up to walking over to a shrub to do what was necessary.

Chadwick picked up the little animal in disgust and practically hurled him towards the shrubbery. 'Dirty little bugger!' he spat, and swayed back into the house to change his trousers, shaking his wet leg as he walked, and abandoning his glass on the table beside the barbecue.

The owners of the house next door, towards Market Street, Riverbanks, took this opportunity to catch Bailey alone, and approached him to make their displeasure known at all the disturbance from their property since the husband had retired. Lucille Sutherland left all the talking to Gerald, as it was his retirement that had been disturbed.

He spoke quite reasonably to Bailey, putting his grievance with simplicity and conciseness to him, but Bailey had been irked by the accusations of Mrs Smallwood. Dipsy may be Chadwick's latest toy, but he was getting rather fond of the little dog's personality, and in his present mood, stood up in his defence rather more vehemently than he would normally have done.

After all, if 'darling Darling' was so precious, why wasn't she penned in securely? – especially if she was on heat. She would attract every dog in the neighbourhood in this condition, and he was sure that innocent little Dipsy wouldn't be the first or the only one to pay heed to his instincts. And he'd bet his shirt the little lady hadn't said 'no', the canine tart.

So he rode roughshod over all of Gerald Sutherland's carefully worded plea for more peace in the future and, although God knows why, announced his intention of taking up the saxophone, as a final nail in the coffin of good neighbourly relations.

As the side gate shut with a sharp clang, it was heard to open again immediately, and a babble of very show-biz chatter hit the party, as the production crew from *Chadwick's Chatterers* entered in a bunch. After their invitation by telephone, they had made calls round, and come in as few cars as possible, so that there were not too

73

many of them restricted to one drink and interminable 'pop'.

Chadwick was, unfortunately, button-holed by Roger and Rita Fairchild of Woodbine Cottage before he could greet them, or even reach the sanctuary of the house, so they made straight for Radcliffe.

Meanwhile, this couple had a grievance to air and Chadwick McMurrough was their target of choice. Their son Rufus had also, by coincidence, been selected to appear in the reality programme *The Glass House*, but had been evicted from it by the public at the end of the first week.

'It should have been him, you know, who won it,' stated Rita baldly. 'It was your fault – you, with your outrageous clothes and your waspish wit.'

'I don't think they should allow gays on that programme. It puts everything skew-whiff, and distorts viewers' opinions,' added Roger, with equal vehemence.

'Oh, piss off, you homophobic old freaks.' Chadwick was really losing a grip of his manners now, and responded without pause for thought.

The couple immediately and, not surprisingly, took umbrage at this – what seemed to them – totally uncalled-for insult, and rushed away in the direction of Nerys and Vince Catcheside from Church Cottage, whom they knew to be of the same opinion as them, as far as Rufus went.

Bailey Radcliffe was absolutely overwhelmed when the entire crew surrounded him at his chef's task, and he greeted them all by name – something it had taken him some time to master, but seemed only polite in the circumstances.

In all, he welcomed five new guests to the party, but was not able to name their partners. All were in attendance, all being Dominic Allencourt, Chadwick's agent; Desmond Hunt-Davies, the programme's director;

74

Neil Summersby, its producer; Daphne Betteridge, its researcher; and finally Melody Crouch, who was responsible for the scripts.

He had been slowly getting to know them since he had taken up with Chadwick, and took this opportunity to meet their other halves. He knew that not all of the crew were particularly fond of Chad, but he liked to feel that they were getting used to his funny little ways and eccentricities, but maybe that was only wishful thinking. Not all of the eyes turned in his direction were full of goodwill.

The Catchesides were deeply involved in discussion with each other, when the Fairchilds pulled up beside them and, after telling the story of what had just occurred near the kitchen entrance, Vince sympathised with them. 'I'm not at all surprised. Nerys and me were just discussing why we came here tonight at all.'

'For me, it was to see how they'd done the inside,' admitted Nerys, going slightly red at the thought that she might get interior design tips from a couple that openly batted for the other side.

'I thought it'd be all pink lace and frills and furbelows,' admitted Vince, with a nasty leer, 'but I reckon they've had someone *normal* do it for them – sort of camouflage for the unwary, in my opinion.'

'I wouldn't be one bit surprised,' agreed Roger Fairchild. 'It was so unfair, putting our Rufus up against someone like that. If they'd said it was fancy-dress,' – this was a reference to the colourful and outrageous dress sense of Chadwick – 'then he'd have taken fancy-dress into the house with him. That McMurrough had an unfair advantage, if you ask me.'

'Bloody shirt-lifters!' spat Vince Catcheside, nevertheless heading towards the bar area in the kitchen for a refill of his glass, while Nerys went across to the barbecue with both their plates for a refill of food.

The production crew had all migrated to where there was a plentiful supply of booze, and as Bailey put pork chops onto the plates held out to him as if beseeching alms, he looked at Nerys Catcheside closely and recognised the all-too-familiar signs. She was sweating slightly, her hands were shaking, and there was real trepidation in her eyes – the typical signs of a homophobe confronting her fear.

Realising that it really was fear of the unknown with her, rather than prejudice and loathing of the incomprehensible, he spoke to her kindly for a minute or two, but it made not a jot of difference to the look of terror behind her eyes, and she scuttled off with the plates, still in awe of the unknown and misunderstood. Here be dragons, indeed.

With a sinking heart, he saw yet another couple approaching him with a zealous and determined look in their eyes, and steeled himself for a further verbal mauling.

This time, his persecutors were the Trusslers from three doors away. Keith put his case for a bit of peace and quiet at night and during the weekends, very reasonably, given the aggravation and disruption to their lives they had put up with. Bailey, however, after his last encounter, and the way the evening was going downhill, in his humble opinion, was not feeling either hospitable or diplomatic.

Just being a faggot, a queer, a gay boy, a figure of fun and derision for most of these people in their nice safe little bubbles, with nothing out of order or upsetting in their cosy little worlds, he was beginning to see red.

He wasn't a square peg in a round hole, and neither was Chadwick. They were square pegs in square holes. It was just that these bigoted, small-minded straights couldn't bring themselves to acknowledge that there was more than one shape of hole. He could feel his anger begin to bubble and seethe.

Finally, it boiled over. He'd spent rather more than a small fortune in Market Darley earlier today to greet these new neighbours and, although he realised that the peacocks had caused some disruption, as had the workmen before them, none of it was directly his fault.

The workmen had just done a normal working day, and he was already in talks to remove the peacocks from the premises. What more could he do?

'You're just a bunch of small-minded, bigoted, thoughtless, intolerant gits!' he shouted, so that more than the Trusslers heard him. 'Here I am, slaving away over a hot barbecue, having spent hours shopping for all the ingredients, and preparing them before you all arrived, and everyone who gets the chance has a go at me.

'Well, I've had enough. Someone else can take over at this bloody fire. I'm going off to get a triple gin and tonic, and you can all go to hell, as far as I'm concerned.'

He realised straight away that Chadwick was on his way back outside, because he heard his voice from the kitchen, clearly saying, 'Right, back to me, now.' He was an egocentric little tyke, but he couldn't help having fallen for him. Maybe he was at a funny age, or something.

As this little incident was unfolding, Chadwick was just emerging from the house in freshly laundered shocking pink trousers, only to be immediately accosted by a very sharply dressed young man smelling strongly of an expensive designer aftershave.

'Good evening, Mr McMurrough. I thought I'd better introduce myself to you, as you'd been civil enough to invite me to your house-warming party, I'm Robin Eastwood from River View, and I'm delighted to meet you. I always watch your chat show.'

'Do call me Chadwick. A pleasure to meet you, too, Robin – if I may make so bold – and I'm so pleased that you like my little show.'

The two positively twinkled at each other, and an invisible message passed between them. As Bailey pushed his way past into the kitchen, Chadwick gave an exaggeratedly theatrical sigh and turned back to his new acquaintance.

'It would seem that something or someone has upset my partner and he's left the barbecue unmanned, so I'd better fill the breach. You go inside and get yourself a drink, then we can have a lovely chat and get to know one another a bit better,' he positively simpered.

Chadwick swayed unsteadily over the flaming coals and charred meat, while Robin Eastwood minced exaggeratedly into the kitchen, his mind working nineteen to the dozen.

In the kitchen, as both Bailey and Robin were testing their drinks, with an exploratory sip in Robin's case, a glass-emptying gulp in Bailey's, there was a scream from outside, and a babble of voices suddenly filled the air.

'What the bloody hell?' queried Bailey, abandoning his glass and running outside to see what all the fuss was about. There was a crowd round the barbecue, and when he elbowed his way through it, he caught sight of Chadwick lying very still on the grass.

'What happened?' he asked, immediately falling to his knees to check whether his partner was still breathing, as Dipsy Daxie also arrived on the scene and began to lick his master's face in concern. Yes! He was unconscious, not dead. But for how much longer? Had he been hit? wondered Bailey, feeling round the back of his head, his hand coming out without any tell-tale blood stains. There were certainly no egg-like lumps present. Had he been poisoned, then?

He must phone for an ambulance immediately, and for the police, for this looked like yet another attempt on the young man's life, and it had to be stopped before he was actually killed.

Rising to his feet and extracting his smartphone from his pocket simultaneously, he shouted as loud as he could, 'Party's over! There's been an accident. I'm calling for an ambulance right now,' while he thought, this is probably no accident to one of these people here. One of these 'guests' wants my Chad dead, and this is his or her fourth attempt. It's got to be stopped before it goes any further.

Market Darley

Harry Falconer was still in his office when the call came through on his mobile. Bailey had wasted no time ringing either his home or his office numbers. Now he had established that there was an ambulance on its way, his next priority was getting in touch with the police as expediently as possible.

Carmichael was just putting on his light jacket to go home, for they had both worked late catching up on necessary paperwork, when the inspector took the call, and a hand raised in his direction immediately halted him.

When the call ended, Falconer gave his sergeant a grave look and said, 'Apparently there's been another attempt on Chadwick McMurrough's life. An ambulance is on its way, and it could be poison this time. Put your jacket on properly, but give Kerry a call on the way over. We have to go to Fairmile Green again, to talk to the people who were there. He collapsed during a house-warming party.

'Luckily, it was by invitation only, and Radcliffe can give us the names of all the people who attended. He had, apparently, just come outside from the house after having had to change his trousers, and he had left his drinks glass on the table by the barbecue. Easy enough, then, for someone to slip something into it on the pretext of examining the food, or chatting to Bailey Radcliffe. Childishly simple, really.'

'Any idea how many of them were at this party?' asked Carmichael, hoping that it had been a fairly intimate affair. He didn't relish the thought of dozens of interviews.

'With the chat show's production team and their partners, nearly thirty; including three children, and one baby, thirty-one in all, but I think we can discount the small fry, so that makes twenty-seven adults.'

'Any with a grudge against McMurrough or Radcliffe?' Carmichael actually had his fingers crossed as he asked this one. Please God let this be a simple case as, with a celebrity involved, it would no doubt father a lot of media interest.

'Oh, just about all of the neighbours, and he's not sure about the production team. McMurrough's not flavour of the month for all of them.'

'Great!' Carmichael had a dreadful sinking feeling in the pit of his stomach that this was going to be a very tricky case indeed, even though no one was dead – yet.

Falconer turned to him, as he drove, and said, 'I know what you're thinking, and I feel exactly the same. This is going to be right in the glare of the public's gaze, and I'm not looking forward to it any more than you are.'

As they pulled up outside Glass House, it was behind a local television news vehicle that had made it there before them. They must have had a tip-off from one of the guests who was 'in the business', so to speak.

Falconer nearly growled out loud, so angry was he, but he squared his shoulders, assembled his 'no comment' features on his face, and got out of the car, Carmichael, with a completely blank expression, on his heels.

Chapter Six

Friday
Market Darley

Chadwick McMurrough's bed in the Market Darley Hospital was surrounded by admiring nurses, as it was not yet visiting time. He had been diagnosed as having been administered a dose of Rohypnol – the date-rape drug – sufficient to incapacitate him for a few hours, but to do no lasting damage, and he was waiting for the doctor to come and pronounce him fit to go home.

He'd already phoned Bailey and given him the approximate time of his discharge, and was spending the intervening interval basking in the limelight from both staff and patients. He was never happier than when surrounded by adoring fans, lapping up their delight in his company, and making him feel special.

There was no chance that he would be detained in the ward any longer, and he was looking forward to getting back home and things getting back to normal. He felt none the worse for his ordeal, and was just anxious to put on his over-the-top clothes again, and get back into the big wide world. He had a show to record tomorrow evening, and he did not want to be distracted from his mental preparations for that.

In the police station, Harry Falconer received a call on his mobile from Bailey Radcliffe about eleven o'clock, informing him that McMurrough had recovered from the latest attempt on his life, and was now at home, deep in preparations for one of his shows that evening.

'We'll be right over to interview him, sir. Thank you for letting me know,' Falconer said, into the phone.

'Oh, I don't know if he'll approve of that. He's deep into his prep for tonight's recording,' replied Bailey, somehow having overlooked this outcome of his call.

'That's what's known as "tough luck", sir. If he wants us to take these attempts on his life seriously, then he's got to allow us to do our job. We're leaving right away; you'd better warn him, so that we're not a nasty surprise. I want him to try to remember everything he can from last night.'

Carmichael looked up at this, and got up from his desk, realising instantly where they were going, and that that going was now.

They both grabbed raincoats from the stand on the way out. As so often happens in this green and pleasant land, the glorious weather had lasted only a short while, and the rain was lashing down now.

Fairmile Green

'Why on earth does he have to come today? I've got to get *au fait* with the details of these guests. For God's sake, I'm not dead. Couldn't he have left it until Monday, when I'll be as free as a bird?'

'Chadders, someone's been trying to kill you, and you want the inspector to delay his investigation by a few days? Do you realise what you're trying to do? You're going to give the killer days of *carte blanche* in which to have another go at you.'

'Don't blow everything out of proportion. I'm sure he

82

won't strike again before next week.'

'How on earth can you be so certain?' asked Bailey.

'Oh, Bails, I expect he's got a life too, and it is Friday night tonight. Bet you your bottom dollar there are no more attempts before Monday.'

'I don't understand why you're so calm.'

'Because the police won't let something serious actually happen to me – not after last night.'

'You're *a* queen, not *the* Queen. I can't see them giving you any special treatment.'

'Well, you'll just have to be extra vigilant on my behalf, won't you, ducky?'

When Falconer's car drew up outside Glass House, it was nose to tail with what looked like the same local television van that had been parked there the night before, and he swore under his breath. 'Come along, Carmichael. Time to run the gauntlet again. We'd better renew our vow of silence.'

The weather was still filthy, and the windows of the local news van had begun to steam up. It simply was too unpleasant to be out and about, trying to do a piece to camera, when there was a positive Niagara streaming down one's collar.

Bailey opened the door quickly and ushered them in, as two other vans arrived almost simultaneously, one from a local paper, the other with the slogan of a national daily along its sides.

'In quick, gents. We don't want to be overrun with reporters, do we? '

'Very *Madame Butterfly* weather,' commented Falconer, to which he only received blank looks.

'One fine day,' he first quoted, then sang, before understanding broke over both countenances.

83

'Lucky we had the barbecue yesterday,' Bailey said, merely as a time-filler, as they entered the living room, only to receive a huge frown of disapproval from Chadwick.

'If we hadn't had the barbecue, someone wouldn't have spiked my drink and I would have been saved a stay in hospital,' whined McMurrough with a pathetic expression. 'It's lucky I wasn't killed.'

'I'm sorry, Chad. I just didn't think. You know what I mean, though. And if we hadn't got all those complaints and grouses over with in one fell swoop we'd have had them coming round in dribs and drabs for days and days, spoiling each one, as they polluted it with their moans and groans.'

'True,' Chadwick had to concede. 'I suppose you two gentlemen want a statement from us.'

'If you please, sir,' replied Falconer, as Carmichael got out his notebook.

'I've made a list of everyone who attended, along with their addresses – I needed the local phone book for that. Couldn't remember which houses some of them professed to come from.'

'That will save us a lot of time, Mr Radcliffe. Thank you very much. Very thoughtful and efficient of you.'

They were interrupted, at this point, by a barrage of knocks on the front door, and someone seemed to have their finger pressed firmly and unrelentingly on the doorbell.

'Damned press again. I'm not answering it. We'll just have to wait until they give up.' Bailey had evidently had more than one round of this un-looked-for attention, and got up from his seat, let down all the blinds, and turned on the lights. 'We'll just have to manage like this, given the circumstances. I hope you don't mind.'

Following this lowering of the blinds, the letterbox

rattled, and they all had a vision of someone looking through to see if they could discern anything of interest from this very limited view. This was followed by what was, now visible in the artificial light, flashes of bright light emanating from the flap.

'I don't believe this. Now they're taking pictures through the letterbox. Well I won't put up with it,' stated Bailey in an angry growl, got up from his seat again and went to a large wooden storage-cum-display unit. From a door in this, he removed a large roll of parcel tape, stalked over to the front door, and taped up the letterbox against further media assault.

'That should sort the nosy buggers out. Now, can I get you chaps a cup of tea or coffee?' With the banishment of further intrusion upon their meeting, Bailey's social manner had returned, and he smiled politely at his guests.

Suddenly Chadwick hissed urgently and uncomprehendingly at him, 'Bails – syrup!' This had the effect of Radcliffe nonchalantly putting a hand to his head, making some sort of calculation, and moving the hand briefly to his left, so that it appeared his whole head of hair moved. If they could work that one out, then good for them – at the moment, he didn't really care.

Both policemen chose coffee, and he left for the kitchen to rustle up a cafetière of the fresh, hot, fragrant liquid. Chadwick tuned in to the present, whereas before, he had been lost in a brown study, and asked them if they'd like to start questioning him.

Bailey was back in only five minutes, and set his tray down on the coffee table. The questioning would have continued, but the sight of Carmichael sweetening his drink caused a hush to fall on the room, and he looked up to find all eyes on him.

'What?'

'How many spoonfuls of sugar did you just put in your

cup?' asked Bailey, fascinated.

'Six.'

'And did you mean to?' So was Chadwick.

'Yes.'

'He always takes six sugars,' confirmed Falconer. 'It's nothing unusual. He's a big lad and he needs to get sufficient energy from somewhere.'

'He certainly *is* big, isn't he?' commented Chadwick, looking the sergeant up and down, and causing him to feel particularly uncomfortable. As he put it to Falconer later, 'It was like he was undressing me with his eyes. I could never be female.'

'Now you know how most women feel a lot of the time,' the inspector had retorted somewhat tartly, shaking his head to dispel the horrible vision his mind had just conjured up, of a female Carmichael, but thinking that, sometimes, it was good for men to know how uncomfortable they made women feel with their searching glances.

From what both McMurrough and Radcliffe told the two detectives, neither of them had noticed anyone lurking near Chadwick's glass when he had left it on the table by the barbecue, and they had both discussed the evening, and decided that this was when something must have been added to his drink.

'We'll just have to do the rounds of the neighbours, then, and see if any of them were more observant,' concluded the inspector. 'Mr McMurrough, when would be a good time to speak to your production team, which I have been reliably informed joined in the house-warming festivities before the unfortunate incident?'

'Not today, if you can help it, because we're recording a show tonight, and they'll be up to their eyes until that's over and done with,' replied Chadwick.

'But it's not on tonight, is it? Have they changed its

slot?' asked Carmichael, anxious not to miss one of his favourite programmes.

'No, it's just recorded in advance. It can sometimes become a bit volcanic, with my, er, temperament,' – here, he had the grace to blush, confirming that his temperament was ninety per cent fictional – 'and the volatility of some of the guests.

'We started going out live, but one of our early guests went ape-shit in the studio, and we had to cut the broadcast to restore order, and eject the person responsible. That may be fairly good for viewing figures in the short term, but it won't be tolerated in the long term, so now we always record in advance, so that the tape can be edited of anything we consider it unwise to broadcast,' he concluded.

'And now, if you've finished with your questions, I have to get on. There are a lot of facts and figures that have to be memorised before I interview my guests, and I need them at the forefront of my mind before we start recording.'

Market Darley

The two detectives ran from the car park to the entrance to the police station, their mackintoshes over their heads as the rain was still coming down like stair rods.

'That's one helluva list he gave us, sir,' Carmichael shouting above the noise of the torrent, as a rumble of thunder sounded in the distance.

'Roberts should be in the office by now. We'll take him along with us this afternoon. I'll get him on the blower to as many of these as he can find in, and sort us out a proper list of visiting times. That should be the most efficient route to take. We can always try those that weren't at home at the end.'

'When are we going to speak to the production crew?' asked Carmichael, holding open the station door to let Falconer enter first, the well-brought up boy.

'Tomorrow morning, I should think. You and I could probably manage that on our own. After all, there are only five of them, I believe. I did catch a quick glance at that list Radcliffe gave you.'

When they shed their wet coats up in the office, there was neither hide nor hair of DC Chris Roberts, and Falconer's temper began to flare. He was not particularly patient with his detective constable, because he seemed to spend an inordinately large amount of time either in hospital or just off work, sick.

And when the detective constable did deign to put in an appearance at the station, spent an inordinate amount of time with his feet up on his desk reading a newspaper, or outside, having a cigarette – Falconer dared not think of using the word 'fag' at the moment – break.

'If that lazy dog's sloped off somewhere, I'll have his guts for garters. Look! There's no sign of a note or a message, either. He'll be swinging the lead somewhere, no doubt. You take a look out of the window and see if you can spot him smoking out there.'

'Then I'll get us both a mug of coffee, sir,' offered Carmichael, anxious to avoid getting caught in the cross-fire and, after a brief glance to confirm that the missing DC was not visible in the car park, went off in the direction of the canteen.

Roberts answered the call after the fourth ring, his voice sounding slightly slushy and abnormal; somehow full of suffering.

'Where the hell are you, Roberts? I've just got back to the office, and there you aren't. Nothing unusual in that, I know but, as far as I know, you're not in hospital just at the moment, so where the hell are you?'

'I'm at home, sir.'

'Why, in the blue blazes are you at home? It's not even lunchtime.'

'It must've been those school talks I did at the end of term,' replied Roberts, cryptically.

'What? Whatever are you talking about, man? Talk sense, for heaven's sake.'

'Incubation times. When I woke up this morning, they were nearly as big as footballs.'

'What incubation? What were as big as footballs? What are you babbling about?'

'I'm a man, sir – a male adult, and this is, apparently, what happens if you get it at my age.'

'Get what? Stop talking in riddles and tell me what's wrong with you now, immediately?'

'Mumps, sir. I must've picked it up doing those road safety and 'stranger danger' talks at the primary schools, before they broke up for the summer holidays. The glands in my neck are also pretty swollen too, and it's agony to try to eat anything.'

'Mumps? I think I realise, now, what are almost as big as footballs.'

'Let me put it this way, sir, if they get any bigger, I think I'll have to walk with a wheelbarrow in front of me.'

'Don't you dare come back to this office until you're completely free of infection, do you hear me?'

'Gotcha, sir.'

When Carmichael re-entered the office carrying two steaming mugs, he asked Falconer if he was really going to have Roberts' guts for garters, now he'd spoken to him.

'No, life has dealt him a much lower blow than that!'

'What's that, sir? Here's your coffee, by the way.'

'Thanks. Our DC Roberts has got mumps. Reckons he

picked it up on his pre-holiday talks to the kids in the local schools.'

'Glad I didn't do them, then. It's a bit late in the year for mumps, though, isn't it?'

'How should I know?'

'Usually March or April time.'

'Whatever. One of the little darlings he has met on his travels has infected him, and he's suffering rather badly from *swellings*.'

'Did you mention a wheelbarrow to him?' asked Carmichael with a grin.

'He suggested one himself. How are you feeling? I've checked myself, and I seem to be a hundred per cent.'

'Fit as a fiddle, sir. Anyway, I had it when I was a kid, and you can't get it twice.'

'Thank God for that. Let's go and get an early lunch, and do this afternoon without appointments. It's not as if any of the addresses are a long way apart, so we can't waste much time. We'll just play it by ear as we won't have the pleasure of Roberts' company.'

Fairmile Green

The two policemen, replete with a canteen lunch, pulled up outside Woodbine Cottage, the residence at the eastern end of the row of houses. 'If we start here, we can work our way along to the other end, then that'll only leave us with the three down Old Darley Passage, and we're done. Any who aren't in at all, we'll have to come back to tomorrow. Are you on duty, then?' the inspector asked Carmichael.

'Course I am, same as you, and we're both off Sunday. You're coming to us for lunch, remember?'

'How could I forget? I'm already looking forward to it,' Falconer replied dishonestly. The real reason he had accepted the invitation was so that he could prevent Heather coming round and cooking for him in his own kitchen – heaven forfend.

'Now, consulting this list, we start with Mr and Mrs Fairchild, then it's Mr and Mrs Catcheside, missing out The Old Smithy – that couple didn't turn up for the party – then Mr and Mrs Warren before we get to Glass House.

'Passing that by, we go on to Mr and Mrs Sutherland, then Mr and Mrs Smallwood, Mr and Mrs Trussler and Mr Eastwood, then we go up to Old Darley Passage for Mr Worsley, Mr Jones, and Mr Westbrook.'

At that moment his mobile rang, and he answered the call to find Bailey Radcliffe on the other end. 'What can I do for you, Mr Radcliffe?' he asked, hoping that nothing else sinister had occurred.

'You'd better add the Innocents to your list, should there be another attempt. I dropped Chadwick off at the studios just now for a technical run, and on the way back, I ran over their cat. The ruddy thing's dead, and they're spitting fire in my direction, so maybe you can expect me to become another target.'

After he'd ended the call, Falconer told his sergeant what had happened, and suggested that they call there anyway, to ask them if they had seen anyone or anything suspicious which could be pertinent to what had been happening in Glass House recently.

Chapter Seven

Fairmile Green

At Woodbine Cottage, the door was opened by a young lad possibly only in his late teens. Falconer gave their names and ranks and asked him if his parents were in.

'They're at work, but you can talk to me if you like,' he offered. 'I'm their son, Rufus, by the way.'

'Did you attend the house-warming party at Glass House last night?' asked Falconer, not wanting to waste his time.

'No I bloody well didn't,' answered the youth, roughly. 'I wouldn't set foot on that cheating poof's property if it was the last house on earth?'

'And which 'cheating poof' would that be?' asked Falconer giving as good as he got.

'That queen, Chadwick sodding McMurrough. It should've been me what won that programme, not him, but he was always playing up for the cameras, simpering at all the cameramen, and dressing like it was some sort of play or summink.

'I was robbed, getting thrown out on the first eviction. Well, I'm going to apply for the *X Factor* next year, and *Britain's Got Talent*. I will get my chance at the high life, with no cheating shirt-lifters like him around to spoil my chances.'

'So you're not a fan of Chadwick McMurrough's, then?'

'No I bleeding well ain't, and that's the truth. I did hear someone's trying to kill him. Well, bloody good luck to them is all I can say.'

And with that charming little speech, Rufus ~~Catcheside~~ Fairchild tried to shut the door in their faces, but Falconer employed an experienced foot to stop him. 'Tell me, sonny, if your parents are at work, why exactly are you lounging around the house during working hours on a weekday?'

'I'm at college in Market Darley, ain't I? I've got no lectures till four, so I can do what I bleeding well want in my free time. It's no business of no nosy copper, so put that in your pipe and smoke it, pal.' The door closed as Falconer removed his obstructing foot, and he turned to his sergeant.

'Make a note, Carmichael. We may have to come back to him. We'll definitely have to come back to speak to the parents, but I think we should add him to our list of possibles. He's certainly hostile enough.

'We shouldn't be long at the next one, either. That's the couple whose cat Radcliffe ran over earlier today, and they hadn't met them before.'

He knocked smartly on the door of The Old Smithy, after there was no answer to his ring on the doorbell, but still the door remained firmly closed. The Innocents were definitely not at home.

'Perhaps they only came home for lunch, sir. If they don't have any children, and they're not retired, people tend to be out at work, if they've got it, during the week.'

'Good point, Sergeant. On we go then.'

A man whom they took to be Vince Catcheside opened the

door to them at Church Cottage. After presenting their credentials, he grudgingly asked them in and led the way into a small sitting room overfull of flower-covered furniture, with equally hectic curtains at the windows, and a patterned carpet on the floor.

It was obvious that he and his wife were over retirement age from their grey hair and wrinkled faces, but there was no evidence of the courtesy of that generation, as they offered their visitors no refreshment.

'You may have gathered that there has been more than one attempt to injure or even kill your new neighbour, Chadwick McMurrough, Mr Catcheside. I'm looking for anything that was seen or heard that could help me find the culprit.

'Both you and your wife were at their house-warming party last night. Did you observe or overhear anything that could be of help to us?'

'Even if I did, I'd keep me trap shut. People like that should be done away with. If whoever it is succeeds, I'll be the first to shake their hand,' Vince Catcheside spat, a look of loathing on his face.

'They ain't natural, them two,' added his wife, looking similarly hostile. 'In some ways, Hitler got it right. They should be rounded up and shot, in my opinion.'

Both detectives were shocked. Neither of them had any idea that such real hatred existed towards gays these days. They had both considered that the days of 'gay bashing' were well and truly over, and this unexpected display of venom was unsettling.

'I don't know whether you've realised it, but homosexuality was decriminalised many years ago, and they do have the right to form civil partnerships these days. They are generally accepted as part of the modern society that has been worked so hard for.'

Falconer knew that he sounded a little pompous, but he

94

was absolutely furious with the bigotry displayed by these two social dinosaurs, and appalled by their prejudice. As he spoke, Carmichael let his breath out in an audible hiss, and turned, of his own accord, towards the front door.

'There's nothing for us here, sir,' he commented, his face a complete blank. 'I suggest we get on with our enquiries elsewhere.'

'Excellent idea, Sergeant.' Without a word of farewell, the two men exited the little house, both of them glad of a breath of fresh air after the tirade of hatred they had just experienced.

As they stood waiting outside the door of Myrtle Cottage they could hear the sound of children's laughter sounding from the other side of it. Their summons was answered by a dishevelled woman, probably in her thirties, with a substance that looked suspiciously like cake-mix in her hair and down the front of her T-shirt.

Discreetly ignoring this probably accidental sartorial addition, Falconer bade her good day, introduced the two of them, and asked if they could come inside for a word or two about what had happened to Chadwick McMurrough the evening before.

Apart from the muttered, 'Little shits,' apparently in judgement of her own children and not the neighbours, she didn't utter a word until she had sat them down in the sitting room. Three children were romping, unchecked, through the house, while a baby, only just crawling, moved slowly across the carpet rather like a snail – its trail, however, being of urine, for it wore no nappy. It was not a restful household.

Before either of them could utter a word, the woman suddenly broke into self-pitying speech. 'Things are a bit fraught around here, as you can see. And I'm surprised no one told you that we left that party almost as soon as we arrived

'Those two unnaturals have got absolutely no empathy towards children. They're so deep in their own twisted world of glamour that they were quite hostile towards my little darlings,' – her face told a different story of how she really felt about her brood – 'and we wouldn't stay there for the kids to be shouted at and generally harassed just for being young and inquisitive.'

'So, were you not there when Mr McMurrough collapsed?'

'Know nothing about it, except what I've learnt on the grapevine.'

'Were you aware that there have been other attacks on Mr McMurrough?'

'No, and I wouldn't be the least interested in finding out about them. No one in this house will cross that threshold again.'

'Thank you for your time and patience,' said Falconer, politely, although he suspected that patience was a quality of which she didn't possess great stores, judging from her facial expression and general air of twitchiness. 'Good day to you – Mrs Warren, isn't it?'

'For now,' was her curt and intriguing answer.

They passed Glass House and approached the next door property, Riverbanks, hoping for a little more success than they had had up to now.

The lady of the house answered their summons, introduced herself as Lucille Sutherland, and advised them that it was her husband they'd want to speak to. 'Only, it's him as has suffered the most. Me, I just get used to things and tune them out, but Gerald's sensitive, like,' she concluded.

Mr Sutherland was to be found in an old leather

armchair in front of an open fireplace, decorously screened now it was summer, keeping himself amused with today's newspaper crossword. He rose to meet them and shook hands. 'I suppose you've come about that incident last night, at next door's moving-in do?' he asked.

'That's right, sir. There have been other attempts to harm Mr McMurrough, and we need to find out everything we can, so that we can apprehend the culprit before anything else, maybe more serious, occurs.'

The inspector was suddenly aware that pomposity was sometimes a little difficult to get rid of, and gave himself a mental shaking to rid himself of this priggish manner of speech.

Carmichael came to his rescue during this slight hiatus. 'Anything at all, Mr Sutherland – maybe something you saw but didn't attach any importance to at the time, maybe something you overheard that perhaps didn't make sense at the time. We need all the help we can get. The police have had enough bad press, and we don't want to add even more to the Force's burden.'

'I can understand that. Damned fine police force we have in this country, but I can honestly say that I saw or heard nothing untoward during my time there, and was as surprised as anyone else when Mr McMurrough suddenly dropped to the ground.'

'If you can just search your memory over the next day or so, we'd be grateful for anything, no matter how small.'

'I'll do my best, but I can't promise anything.'

At that point, Lucille entered the room with a laden tea tray and proved a very welcome distraction. As she poured from the pot she told the three men to take a plate and help themselves. The rock cakes were home-made, as were the individual treacle tarts, and Carmichael's eyes positively lit up.

It was at least two hours since he'd had lunch and

97

substantial though that meal had been, he was already hungry again. Keeping such a large machine fuelled was a constant challenge to him, and he took every opportunity he could to stoke up his engine.

Lucille Sutherland handed out brimming cups, and her husband started out on an explanation he had not been pressed to give, but felt it only fair that his feelings be known, about what had been happening next door. Apart from that, if he didn't say anything, Lucille would wonder why, as it had been almost his sole topic of conversation for months, now.

'We've had a lot of trouble with noise nuisance from The Orchards,' he began.

'The Orchards?' queried Falconer.

'Oh, that was the old name of next door. Got the fancy name Glass House now, probably after that awful TV programme the young one appeared in,' continued Gerald. 'People say he's got his own chat show now, but I couldn't be bothered to watch anything so facile. And it's on pretty late. We usually go to bed early.

'Not that we get to sleep early any more, if at all. But I'll start at the beginning,' he said, seeing the look of puzzlement on both policemen's faces.

'I retired some months ago, and I was looking forward to having time to call my own, and some peaceful days pottering around the house and the village. I no sooner retire, than those two must have bought the house next door, which had been for sale, although we had no idea it was on the market, and the noise started.

'It was in a terrible state when they must have bought it. Yes, it's a good-sized house, but the little Darle runs below its foundations, and only a cash buyer would have done. Anyway, the workmen moved in, and that was the end of peace and quiet.

'It needed everything doing – new electrics, new

plumbing, new bathrooms, new kitchen, new windows – and what a palaver it's been. Have you seen the amount of glass in that house? There was some re-plastering, and rooms knocked into one another, and all the redecorating, with heaven knows what else into the bargain.

'They had to have re-pointing done, insulation; you name it – the works. The noise was indescribable, and it went on from eight-thirty in the morning to six at night; thankfully only on weekdays. The men didn't work Saturdays.

'I thought I'd go out of my mind, and took to seeking sanctuary in the little yards that lie behind the shops in the main streets with my paper. At least things weren't so loud there, and I could hear myself think.

'Then it stopped, and they moved in, and I thought I'd finally get my peace and quiet. The next thing you know, the maniacs have installed a whole herd of peacocks – I'm afraid I don't know the collective noun for the birds, but 'herd' does it for me.

'All we've had ever since is their incessant cries, which sound like cries for help. I don't know if the noise abatement officer can help, or even if they're considered pets.'

'I'm sure that Mr McMurrough and Mr Radcliffe have also suffered from loss of sleep. They certainly had bags under their eyes when I last saw them. I'll have a word when I next speak to them about what their plans are for the creatures and, may I suggest that, in the meantime, maybe you start wearing earplugs. I know it's not the ideal solution, but you might get a little more rest.'

Falconer was as sympathetic as he could be, but couldn't deny or confirm whether keeping peacocks could be classed as a criminal offence.

'Do you know, I never thought of that. It would be a sort of interim stage wouldn't it? Lucille, you can nip out

99

to the pharmacy in Market Street as soon as these gentlemen are on their way, and buy us a couple of pairs.'

The inspector drained his cup, at the same time noticing that Lucille Sutherland was looking, in what appeared to be fascination, in Carmichael's direction. He turned his head, to see what had caught her attention so, and his expression froze.

The younger man had availed himself freely of the available refreshments, but without prior warning about Lucille Sutherland's home-baking. He had encountered problems with both offerings, but had sat in silence, quietly fighting them, to try to extract some sort of nourishment.

His shirt front and lap were covered in rather large crumbs – some of which were more akin to lumps – of rock cake. The lady took their name as their nature, and cooked them accordingly.

The treacle tarts, he had had much more difficulty with, as she only ever added the minimum of breadcrumbs, leaving the golden syrup still runny. He had evidently tried to eat one of these first, and a number of pieces of rock cake were stuck to his chin and one cheek; his tie was also a nest, this time for currants from the rock cakes, and his hands were stuck together with the golden trap.

All in all, Falconer decided, he looked like a child who has had a very messy teatime. 'Do you think my sergeant could go somewhere to clean himself up?' he asked of his hostess, trying to keep a straight face, and noticing that while the wife and he had listened politely to Gerald's tale of woe, Carmichael had silently emptied both plates. It served him right!

'We don't have any facilities downstairs like modern homes, but he's welcome to go upstairs to the bathroom and have a bit of a wash,' said Lucille, now noticeably trying to suppress a grin of amusement. 'Go on up and have a bit of a tidy-up, Sergeant.'

When Carmichael once again resembled a grown-up, he accompanied the inspector to the door of Green Gates, in search of the Smallwoods, and their knock was answered, after only a short pause, by a woman who appeared to be in her thirties – so, she was not out at work.

Once inside, both were examined minutely by the nose of a small – but not as small as Carmichael's two – dog, which they were informed was a Shih Tzu who went by the name of Darling.

'I've been passionately fond of dogs for years,' explained Darling's owner, 'and I finally took my courage in both hands, resigned from my day job, and bought a bitch for breeding.' Carmichael winced at the word 'bitch'. Earlier, at the Fairchilds' house, his face had almost gone into spasm at the bad language of Rufus, the only family member at home. He did not approve of what he referred to as 'cursing'.

'She's just come into her first season, and I had arranged for a stud to come and cover her this morning. That's why I didn't intend to go to the party at Glass House last night – I felt I needed to keep an eye on her and keep her company – and why I'm so furious with the couple who live there.'

'Do go on,' Falconer encouraged her. Carmichael had abandoned his note-taking in favour of playing with the little animal, and the inspector coughed pointedly to recapture his attention.

'Sorry, sir.'

'My husband is away on business at the moment, so it was just the two of us yesterday – Darling and I, you understand. I went upstairs for a shower to try to cool down, as it was such a hot day, and when I got back downstairs, that foul miniature sausage dog that they'd just acquired had managed to get into my garden under the fence, and was having his wicked way with my poor darling Darling.'

That was one 'darling' too many for Carmichael, and he had to stop for a minute, to rest his pen, while he sorted it out in his mind.

'It was mid-evening by then, and I just grabbed him and marched round to the party – I was invited, after all, so I wasn't gate-crashing – but that was exactly what I did. I fair crashed through the side gate, having got no answer at the front door, located the owners over at the barbecue, just dumped the dog down, and vented my spleen on them.

'Of course, I let the stud come this morning, but if she has a litter of cross-bred pups, I shall be consulting my solicitor as to whether I have any come-back under the law. This is my job now, and the pups will provide my only income. It was a risky business in the first place, and with this sodding sausage-shaped seducer, I could be in hot water, money-wise.

'I won't even be able to advertise their imminent birth, so that I can get pre-whelp orders, unless the vet's got a scanner that can distinguish whether she's carrying Shih Tzu or cross-bred pups.'

'You have all my sympathy, Mrs Smallwood. So you weren't at the party very long, then?'

'Only a few minutes. Just long enough to drop off – literally – the canine equivalent of Casanova and have my say, then I stalked back here and had a good cry, hoping my poor Darling wasn't yet pregnant.'

Next door, at Fairview, the Trusslers were obviously out at work, as was their next target, Mr Eastwood, who resided at River View in Market Street.

'We've only got three more to do today,' announced Falconer, 'if we don't go back to any who were not in and, if they're at work, we'd have more chance of catching them on a Saturday morning than we would on a Friday afternoon.

'There's a pub down the other end of the High Street with an all-day licence. Shall we call in there first, to see if we can't get a cup of coffee to warm us up? This rain really makes you feel chilly, doesn't it? We can cross over to the other side by the footbridge halfway down.'

Carmichael accepted the offer with alacrity. He might not long ago have had a cup of tea, but another drink was always acceptable to him, no matter how soon after the last.

The pub was The Goat and Compasses, and they did serve coffee – freshly filtered – so the two detectives took a seat in the nearly empty bar and prepared for a short break, both physically and mentally, from their questioning.

'Do you know how pubs with this name came by it?' asked Falconer, always willing to share the bits of junk and trivia that built up in his head.

'Can't see any sense in the name, myself. What on earth's a goat going to do with a compass, let alone a set of them? Seems daft to me.'

'That's because originally there was no goat, nor any compasses. Neither of them existed.'

'How's that, then. How could it have got its name if the two things mentioned in it didn't exist?' Carmichael's interest had been sparked.

'Because the name is actually a bastardisation, over time, of "God encompasseth us",' explained the inspector, smiling happily, as light dawned for his sergeant.

'That's amazing, sir. I'd never have guessed that in a million years. How do you know things like that?'

'I guess my brain's just a hoarder. I can't seem to throw anything away, and the damned thing's full of such useless facts.'

'Fascinating, I'd say. Don't knock it.' Carmichael was, as he would have described it himself, 'well impressed'.

It had only been spitting when they entered the pub, and the rain had completely stopped by the time they came out and headed for Old Darley Passage, which they knew led to Darley Old Yard, one of the places to which Gerald Sutherland admitted he had fled from the noise next door.

Their initial port of call was at the first of a pair of small semi-detached houses which proclaimed itself to be '2B', where they hoped to find one Mr Westbrook. He, unfortunately, proved to be another potential witnesses who had a job and was, consequently, not at home halfway through a Friday afternoon, and apparently didn't even knock off early for the weekend.

'Bet you a fiver he's self-employed,' said Carmichael, out of the blue.

'What makes you think that?'

'Simply because he hasn't come home early. If you work for yourself, you put in all the hours available, because you don't know when the work's going to dry up and leave you without an income.'

'Now you're the one with the interesting facts. Where did you get that one from?'

'My brothers,' replied Carmichael, with a grin.

'I should've known. Let's try next door. Good grief, look at the name sign for this one – "Or Not 2B". I've never seen anything like that before.'

'Very Shakespearian,' commented Carmichael, causing Falconer to give him a thoughtful stare. He wouldn't have considered his sergeant to be a man who would take any notice of Shakespeare's works, but he must be wrong.

'Did *Hamlet* at school, sir. And me mum loves the

plays. Remember, my middle name's from *Twelfth Night*, then there's my siblings.'

Very unusually, 'Davey' – an adopted forename for an easier progress through life – Carmichael had siblings named Romeo, Hamlet, Mercutio, Juliet, and Imogen. There was also a Harry, which was presumed to be an homage to one of the Henry plays, and his own given forenames were Ralph (pronounced 'Raif') Orsino.

That, at a quick check, covered *Romeo and Juliet*, *Hamlet*, *Twelfth Night*, and *The Taming of the Shrew*.

'However could I forget?' replied Falconer, 'Having been at your wedding and Harriet's christening, they are etched indelibly on my memory, now that you mention them.'

They suddenly realised that they were standing in front of a still-closed door, and that, after all this time, it was unlikely to be answered. They had another no-show to add to tomorrow's list. 'Come on, sergeant, let's try across the road, and see if we have better luck there.'

They certainly had more luck, but there was no definitive answer to whether it was good or bad. The door to Lane House was answered by a man in scruffy and food-stained clothes, who seemed to be hanging on to the door itself to keep upright.

'Mr Worsley?' enquired the inspector, not making any rash judgements about the figure that confronted them.

'Thassright,' replied the man. 'Wha' c'n I do fer you gen'lemen?'

That was plenty for Falconer to judge from, and he judged that the man whom they wished to question was undoubtedly very drunk, and had already reached the slurring and staggering stage.

Carmichael had also come to the same conclusion, and thought that they were unlikely to get anything of import out of him in this state.

'D'you wanna c'me in?' asked the man, who had begun to sway and grin inanely at them.

Carmichael stepped bravely into the breach, took Darren Worsley firmly by an arm and marched him into the house, eventually depositing him in what looked like the comfiest chair in a very mixed bunch.

The place was a mess, with discarded containers from takeaways mixed with empty drinks glasses and newspapers everywhere. There were several beer cans over near a wastepaper basket, a nest of wine bottles on the floor, and an open whisky bottle on the coffee table.

'Take a sheat and shtate yer bis'n'ss,' the man slurred, closing one eye to bring them more sharply into focus. I was jus' hav'n' a li'l snifter. D'yer wan' one?'

'No thank you,' replied Falconer, then determined to state his business, in the hope that the man could still recall the previous evening. 'I understand that you attended a house-warming party at Glass House yesterday,' he began.

'Where? Don' know wha' yer talkin' abou',' their potential witness replied, pouring himself a further three fingers of spirit.

'Used to be called The Orchards,' added Carmichael helpfully.

'Home o' tha' stinkin' unfaithful bastard Radcliffe. Dumped me, yer know. Jus' when things were goin' well. Took off with tha' snotty little guttersnipe McMurr-urr-urrough, an' lef' me high 'n' dry.'

'You used to be Bailey Radcliffe's partner?' asked Falconer, aghast that this seemingly alcoholic wreck could ever have had anything to do with the fastidious Radcliffe.

'Wor? You di'n guess I was an "iron" too?'

'What's an iron?' asked Carmichael, in all innocence.

'Iron hoof. Poof,' Falconer informed him, *sotto voce*.

106

'I wasn' always li' this, yer know. I used to be respect … respect … shober, yer know.'

'And can you, then, tell me what you remember from yesterday evening at the, er, The Orchards?'

'Did I go there?' Worsley's face screwed up with the effort of memory.

'Ah, we'll come back another time, sir. You seem rather tired today. We'll leave you in peace to have a rest, and come back tomorrow morning.' There was no point in wasting any more time on this lush. He wouldn't talk any sense until he'd had a chance to sleep off his binge.

'Lovely to shee you. Come back anytime. I'll be 'ere. Go' nowhere else to go.' Worsley waved a limp hand in farewell, and applied himself to his glass again. For now, he was a lost cause.

As they walked back to the car, Falconer was in thoughtful mood. 'I can hardly believe that Radcliffe was a previous partner of that drunken sot,' he said judgementally.

'He probably wasn't always like that, sir. Maybe the break-up turned him to drink.' Carmichael was more forgiving.

'And maybe it didn't. Maybe it just exaggerated an already bad habit.' Falconer was not letting up: he'd taken a scunner to Worsley, and would not be deflected from his newly formed opinion.

'This afternoon's been a total waste of time. Hardly anyone in, and the only one we got to talk to couldn't talk back and make any sense. In fact, the whole day's been a bit of a washout. Nobody saw or heard anything, apparently.'

'Or so they say, sir. And we have collected a load of grudges against the couple,' the sergeant said soothingly.

'They wouldn't do that if they were responsible for the attacks.' Falconer was determined to be pessimistic.

107

'Or maybe they're just double-bluffing us, sir.'

'Hey, you could be right. Maybe it was one of the people we've spoken to. And if it's not, perhaps it'll turn out to be one of the ones we interview tomorrow morning.'

Carmichael's quiet words had worked, and he was now turned more towards optimism. His glass was half-full again, instead of half-empty, which was more than could be said for Mr Worley's – that was almost brim-full after yet another refill.

Chapter Eight

Fairmile Green

Chadwick slammed down the phone in its cradle and cursed. 'Shit!'

'What's up, Chadders?' called Bailey's voice from the kitchen.

'Bloody technical problems at the studio. Tonight's recording's had to be cancelled, and rescheduled for tomorrow evening. Damn and blast it! I've spent most of the day learning all the facts and figures and getting myself into the right frame of mind to do a real humdinger, and they cancel at the last minute.'

'Well, you won't have forgotten everything by tomorrow evening, will you? It's not the end of the world.'

'Yes it is. I'm bored, and you know how I can't stand being bored. And I even went in earlier to talk to the team about some of the stuff I wanted to do 'off the cuff'. There certainly weren't any technical problems on the dry run.'

'I know you went in. I was the one who took you over there, then went back and picked you up later. I didn't think you'd even bother coming back.'

'Just as well that I did, as they've cancelled the whole bloody thing. I'd have been left at a right loose end there, otherwise. I know! We'll go down to the pub. We were too late to go the other night, so we'll go tonight. Now people know I'm here, actually living in the village, there should be quite a gathering of the fans – geddit – gathering of the fans, instead of clans?'

'Oh, I get it all right. You need an infusion of adulation, and you're not going to get that at the studio now, so I've got to be dragged out to the village pub so that you can go in search of people who'll be prepared to spend all evening worshipping their current televisual god.'

'Got it in one. Remember, it's *all* about *me.*' Radcliffe had hit the nail right on the head, as far as McMurrough was concerned 'I'm going upstairs to put on something lovely,' chirruped the Little Princess, and minced out of the room.

'Well, I hope you don't expect me to change just for the village pub, 'cause I won't,' Bailey called after his figure, which was now disappearing up the stairs. 'And when I got back from the shops earlier, who the hell were you on the phone to? You looked like the cat that'd got the cream!'

'Can't remember,' shouted back Chadwick, but he smiled a secret smile. Some things a girl just had to keep to herself.

On the second step, the phone rang again, and he backtracked to answer it. The call was for him and did not last long, but his Cheshire cat smile got even broader as the call progressed. By the time the call ended, he looked like he'd won a multiple rollover on the Euro Millions lottery. Everything really was coming up roses.

When he wafted downstairs later, Bailey suppressed both a shudder and a chuckle. 'What in the name of God are you wearing, young Chadders?'

'A kaftan and loons,' replied the younger man – there was nearly thirty years between them.

'Why loons, for heaven's sake?'

'Because retro is highly trendy now.'

'Look here, I remember loons when they came round the first time, and they weren't trendy *then*. They were a pain in the butt, with those hugely wide leg bottoms that could find any puddle within a hundred yards and take a drink from it.'

'Shut up, granddad, and get with it. These are absolutely the newest craze.'

'In your dreams, soft lad. You look like a superannuated hippie who's managed the impossible and travelled in time.'

'Not enough time to actually catch you looking young. And anyway, I'm allergic to dinosaurs.'

'Cheeky young pup. I'll box your ears for you.'

'Syrup, Bails.'

'Syrup of figs, my big fat hairy arse, you lying hound. My toupee is perfectly straight. I've just checked it in the mirror.'

'Hey, it's coming on to rain,' called Chadwick, looking outside. 'Let's go mad and wear our Mickey Mouse rain capes. You remember? The ones we bought in Disneyland Paris when there was that awful storm.'

'Do we have to?'

'Of course we do. We're the nearest thing to royalty this village has got.'

The Goat and Compasses had very few customers when they arrived. Not only was it quite early in the evening but, on a Friday, many of the regulars went into Market Darley in search of more lively night life.

No one, at this time, recognised McMurrough, and he sat on a stool looking gloomily at the optics, when the door opened and admitted his ex, Gareth Jones, late home from work and stopping off for a well-earned pint.

He stopped in his tracks when he saw who was sitting at the bar, and exclaimed, 'Can't I go anywhere in this village without seeing you?'

'Well, you did come to my house yesterday for a party. You can hardly expect not to catch at least a glimpse of me in my own home.'

'That's fair enough, but what's a celebrity like you doing wasting his time in a dump like this? I'd have thought you'd have somewhere much more glamorous to have a drink in.'

'Watch it, Gareth,' warned the landlord, as Chadwick replied,

'You bitch! I'll drink where I sodding well like. I don't need your permission to visit my own local.'

'It used to be *my* local, but if you're going to start coming here regularly, I'm going to call in at one of the other villages if I want a drink on the way home from work in future. I don't want to keep bumping into a cheating bastard like you.'

'That's mutual, Gareth, I can assure you. You go where you want, but I reserve my right to visit my local pub for a drink when we don't fancy driving.'

'I'm just surprised you haven't hired a chauffeur by now, or is that your new bloke's job? No, I forgot – he's as old as the hills, isn't he?'

'You mind your mouth, Jones, or I'll relieve you of a few teeth.' This was from Bailey Radcliffe who, up till now, hadn't even turned round.

'You and whose army, old man?' taunted Gareth.

'That's enough of that. I'll have no rough stuff in my establishment. I suggest you have your drink at home, Gareth. These two gentlemen were here first,' called out the landlord, wanting to get in his two-penn'orth before there was a physical fight.

'Oh, that's right, throw me out. I suppose they've got more in their wallets than me.'

'You know that's not the reason. I'm a fair man, and if you'd been here first, I'd have asked them to leave. Now be a good chap and cut along, now.'

Gareth Jones stormed out of the pub and set off, in a foul mood, for Old Darley Passage and home. That unpleasant incident had certainly *not* made his day.

As the evening progressed, quite a few more customers turned up, and they were fans of *The Glass House* and *Chadwick's Chatterers*, so McMurrough got his circle of admirers, and was happy again.

Bailey was, in all honesty, bored. He'd witnessed too much of this to think it a good thing, as Chadwick's ego was ever-expanding, making him, after such a session, almost impossible to live with.

'I think I'll toddle on home, now,' he announced, interrupting Chadwick's assembled fans.

'I'll see you off,' replied Chadwick. 'Just wave you down the street.'

'That's very sweet of you.'

'I know, but I just wanted to prove to you that I could walk away from an adoring crowd. I'll be back in a minute everyone. Powder your noses or get another round in – whatever. I won't be long.'

The couple exited the bar arm in arm, Chadwick looking back and blowing a kiss to his fans. 'See you in no time at all,' he called after them, as they went out into the High Street.

And he was. He was gone less than ten minutes, during which time his fans had hardly noticed the passage of time, as they enthusiastically discussed their favourite scenes from their beloved one's career, and got another round in.

'There, you see, I'm back already,' he said as greeting.

113

'Back in a jiffy, just like I said,' and he settled down in his seat at the head of the table ready, once more, to give audience to his faithful.

Market Darley

Harry Falconer had been dozing under the uncomfortably furry – at this time of year – blanket of five cats, when his landline phone rang at half-past eleven. Coming fuzzily back to consciousness, he batted the cats away and picked up the handset, to find Bob Bryant, the desk sergeant, at the other end of the line.

'Sorry to disturb you so late, but there's been a death in Fairmile Green, and I knew you'd be interested, as you've already had dealings with the victim. You might want to give Carmichael a ring as well.

He did this without delay, and immediately went out to his car, feeling vaguely depressed.

Fairmile Green

On the drive over to Fairmile Green, Falconer's mind went over and over what he had just been told. Bailey Radcliffe's body had been found floating in the waters of the Little Darle in the middle of the village. And it had been Chadwick McMurrough who had found this horror.

It gave so much more importance to what they had found out during their visits today, and Carmichael had been right – they really did have a lot of motives and, if he wasn't mistaken, there'd be a lot more before this investigation was over. He was, of course, assuming that Bailey Radcliffe had been murdered, and not just suffered a fatal accident.

As the nearest to the village, he was the first to arrive

on the scene. Carmichael had further to come from Castle Farthing and Doc Christmas, the FME, even further, from Fallow Fold – a good ten miles.

He parked his car outside the craft shop in the High Street. At least with the twin roads being so wide, there were no double yellow lines to worry about. He left his car just opposite a small group of people who had gathered beside the infant river, and appeared to be staring at something that was lying on the bank.

They were. The crowd parted as Falconer arrived, holding out his warrant card for inspection by anyone who had not yet received a visit from him, and he became aware of the soaking wet body of a totally bald man, lying just short of the second footbridge down from the pub.

By his side knelt a tragic figure, sobbing piteously and clutching what, at first sight, looked like a guinea pig, but which proved, on closer inspection, to be the dead man's toupee, which had never fooled anyone before, and certainly wouldn't now.

'I didn't know what to do about it,' said Chadwick in strained tones, holding up the bunch of 'real human hair' that had once adorned his partner's head. 'It looked so pathetic, just floating there that I had to fish it out. It was part of who he was, and I couldn't just abandon it. I can't believe I'll never see his beautiful brown eyes smiling at me again. We had so many plans.'

Falconer had already taken in the scene when Carmichael arrived. The sergeant must've driven like the very devil to have made it so quickly to Fairmile Green. 'If you don't mind, sir,' the inspector said to McMurrough, 'I'll get my sergeant to take you home, and I'll come along to talk to you later.'

Carmichael, who had just got out of his car, was quick on the uptake, and came over to collect the bereaved. 'But I can't just leave him here,' wailed Chadwick, resisting

Carmichael's hand on his arm.

'He's gone, sir. He's not here any more. You won't be leaving him. He's already left.' Falconer said this gently but decisively. The last thing he needed was the recently bereaved, when the cold, clinical eye of Philip Christmas, the medical man, was assessing the scene. His professional detachment would probably send McMurrough over the edge, he thought, as he watched the two men walk away down the road.

Doc Christmas joined him about ten minutes later, as eager as a puppy to be let loose on the body. 'Good evening, Harry. What have you got for me this time? Anything interesting?'

'Were you told this was the partner of Chadwick McMurrough?'

'I was. I'm hoping to meet the star myself. I'm sure we can come up with some excuse, even if it's just asking him if his partner took any regular medication.'

'You are blatant, aren't you?' Falconer was flabbergasted.

'I'm no different to your average celebrity-hunter,' he replied, coolly, but with a small grin to show that he appreciated the black comedy of the situation – a man of his standing and education chasing after meeting a chit of a boy, with nothing but outrageous clothes and a similarly outrageous personality in his favour.

'Would you like to examine the body, now?' asked Falconer, flashing his eyes at the doctor, to show he understood the meaning of his quick grin.

Christmas was already on his hands and knees beside the earthly remains of Bailey Radcliffe, his hands at the back of the dead man's head.

'There's a lump I can feel here the size of an egg – a sure sign of trauma from a blunt instrument. It's too dark here for me to take a proper look, so I'll have to wait till I get back to the morgue to take a proper look, but I'd say we were looking at a murder.

'If someone belted him on the back of the head and rendered him unconscious, it wouldn't take long, or much effort, to tip him into the river and hold his head under the water. Unconscious people tend not to struggle.'

'But no one had anything against Bailey Radcliffe to my knowledge, and all of the other attempts have been made on Chadwick McMurrough,' countered Falconer.

'Nevertheless, it's Radcliffe body that has been pulled out of the water. I've noticed the lighting isn't very good along this street. They haven't got the sodium lamps we have in the towns, they've still got the dim, old-fashioned ones. Has it crossed your mind that it may have been a case of mistaken identity?'

'Well, poor lighting aside, they both seem to have had on identical rain capes. If someone saw McMurrough go into the pub – maybe he went in behind Mr Radcliffe – then maybe they just assumed it was he who had come out,' interjected Falconer.

'What with the steeling of the nerves to carry out such an attack,' continued Doc Christmas, 'they must have just taken it for granted that it was McMurrough that they'd clobbered and, by the time they'd turned him over to get him submerged, there was simply nothing they could do about it. It was far too late to think of something like that – simply no way back, especially if whoever it was, was worried he – or she – had been seen.'

'So if I consider the theory of mistaken identity,' said Falconer, with calculation in his voice, 'then someone's still got it in for Chadwick McMurrough.'

'Surely not so soon after this happening?' Doc Christmas was horrified at such a thought.

'I don't know. The earlier attacks were crude and ineffectual, but that was more luck than judgement. And whoever it was, had to get into the house to set some of the traps. That takes some nerve. I reckon we'll have to tell Mr McMurrough to keep a sharp eye out, trust no one, and we'll make sure that a patrol car passes the house at least once an hour.'

'Is there no one who could come and stay with him for a while?' The FME was beginning to sound like a mother hen.

'Actually, his mother doesn't live too far away. I've actually met her. Perhaps he'd consider asking her over to stay with him for a while. At least we can keep her off our list of suspects. I'll be off down there now, and suggest the idea when I get there,' the inspector declared as he walked across to his parked car, on his way to join his sergeant.

The door of Glass House was opened to him by a somewhat calmer Chadwick McMurrough who was now in dressing gown and slippers, evidently fresh from the shower.

As he ushered Falconer into the living room, he became aware of two things. One, was the figure of an immaculate young man, quite at home in one of the big armchairs. The other was a strong scent of cigarette smoke in the air. Carmichael was nowhere to be seen, which was a bit puzzling, but he kept his peace.

McMurrough immediately sprayed an air freshener towards the ceiling, and said, 'Sorry about the fug. I haven't smoked for ages, and then I remembered, from last night, that Robin did – this is Robin Eastwood, by the way, from Market Street – and I knew I needed to have some company, otherwise I'd go off my head.

'I gave him a ring and told him what happened, and he very kindly turned up with a bottle of very good malt and three packets of Benson and Hedges. We met at our barbecue house-warming, in case you're wondering.'

'Fags for the faggot,' interjected Eastwood lazily and, unexpectedly in Falconer's opinion, the young householder didn't take offence, even though they had known each other only since the previous evening.

Falconer held out a hand in greeting, only to have own grasped in what felt like the body of a damp, cool fish. 'I called at your house earlier today to speak to you,' said Falconer, 'But you were out.'

'That's work for you, but there's no rest for the wicked, is there?' Eastwood replied smoothly.

'And what do you do?'

'Oh, this and that. You know – whatever it takes to keep a roof over my head and food in my belly.'

Falconer didn't consider that sixty fags and a bottle of malt actually came under the heading of 'keeping body and soul together', but he made no comment. 'Can you tell me how you came to find Mr Radcliffe's body?' asked the inspector as gently as he could.

Chadwick's eyes welled with fresh tears and he made a visible effort to pull himself together. Mr Eastwood kept himself busy with lighting another cigarette and pouring the both of them a fresh drink.

'Bailey went home early because I think he'd had enough of my fans and their fawning ways.'

'I thought you were recording a programme tonight.'

'That's just it. I was supposed to be, but I got a call to say that it had been delayed till tomorrow evening because of some sort of technical problems, so I suggested we went down to the local. I was bored, you see. Bails knows – knew – how bad for me that was.

'Anyway, I think he'd had enough,' he continued, taking another cigarette from the pack offered to him, and lighting up unthinkingly and, after a long drag, appeared ready to continue with his story.

This, however, was postponed by the entry of Carmichael and a tiny Dachshund, holding a stick between them. Falconer had been aware that there was something missing when he had first arrived, and that that something was his sergeant, but the cigarette smoke and the presence of Robin Eastwood had completely knocked him off track.

And the appearance of Carmichael, attired as he was tonight, had a similar effect. He hadn't been able to see him clearly before because of the poor street lighting, and he was somewhat distracted with the corpse. For a moment or two he was speechless.

'Hello, sir. I'm just keeping Dipsy from under anyone's feet,' he said, grinning with pleasure at his new canine companion.

'Good for you Carmichael,' the inspector managed to croak, having recovered his voice. 'Perhaps you could take him back where you've come from, so that you don't interrupt Mr McMurrough, who is going through the circumstances in which he found the body of his partner.'

'Sorry, sir. Come on Dipsy, boy. Let's go back into the other room and play fetch again.' Really, Carmichael was as easy to amuse and distract as a puppy. 'Then get yourself back in here to take notes, Sergeant,' he shouted after Carmichael's departing back.

'Mr McMurrough?' Falconer urged his witness, as his colleague re-entered the room and made himself nearly invisible in one of the feather-stuffed armchairs and tried manfully to take notes from this ludicrous position.

'OK, where was I? That's it – Bailey left early, and I told the fans at the table that I'd just wave him off. It seemed only polite, and it gave me a minute or two away from the incessant questions.

'I went back into the pub, and I didn't leave until closing time. I was walking down the High Street, on the river side rather than that of the shops, when I saw something floating in the water.

'I had no idea what it was, but it looked like a small animal, and I thought I'd better try to get it back to dry land. I'd had a few sherbets by then, and I wasn't really thinking straight.

'But, as soon as I caught hold of it, I could see exactly what it was. Then I became conscious of Bailey, lying face down just a few feet away. When I had a proper look, it looked like his wig had caught on a branch of wood, but his body hadn't floated further downstream because it was caught up on a dumped supermarket trolley – and there isn't even a supermarket in the village.' This last was said in utter disbelief that someone would go to the trouble of bringing such a thing to Fairmile Green just to throw it in the Little Darle.

'Can you believe someone would throw something like that into a tiny rivulet like that? There's nowt so queer as folk – not even queers, Inspector.

'You can't believe how poignant it was, down on my haunches beside the river, with a soaking wet wig in my hands, and my future just a few feet away, drowned and no more.'

After about a quarter of an hour of desultory questioning in which nothing new was disclosed, Falconer alerted Carmichael, preparatory to leaving, and told Chadwick about the hourly check by patrol cars, warning him to be extra vigilant of his own safety.

'What about having your mother over to stay for a while, just until we've got this thing wrapped up, and the culprit behind bars?'

'Are you out of your mind? Have that raddled, nosy old gannet actually stay in my house – not a chance. Actually, Robin here has said he'll stay over, just in case I can't sleep, and I've got an alarm system, though I haven't used it yet. We'll just have to take it from there.'

When they reached the kerb where their cars were parked, Falconer put a hand on his sergeant's shoulder to delay him getting into his vehicle. 'One moment, Carmichael. Has anyone made any comment about the way you're dressed this evening?'

'No, sir,' replied the sergeant, looking down at his body in puzzlement. 'Is there something wrong with it?'

'Allow me to enumerate your garments. You have on a pair of hot pink and bright orange paisley-patterned knee-length shorts. Above, you are attired in a lime green T-shirt with the words "The Stranglers" on it. Below, you are sporting fluorescent yellow flip-flops. Does that seem appropriate attire for a detective sergeant attending a murder scene?'

'It was late when you phoned, sir, and it is quite warm. I was just lying around in what I changed into after work. I didn't think to go upstairs and put on something different. I thought it was more important I got to the scene of the crime as quickly as possible.'

'Which you certainly did. You must have driven like Lewis Hamilton to get here so quickly. May I suggest that, in the future, you consider the suitability of what you are wearing before going out of your front door, and drive at a speed that won't put your name on the statistics that record those who died on the local roads this summer?'

'Yes, sir. Sorry, sir. But I got his autograph before you arrived.'

There was a moment's silence, then Falconer took a deep breath. 'Are you telling me that, after escorting a man home who has just found the murdered body of his life partner, you actually had the brass-necked cheek to ask him for his autograph?'

'It was nice and quiet. It seemed like a good time to me,' replied the sergeant, surveying the inspector quizzically.

'And did you really think it was appropriate to turn up to the scene of a death with "The Stranglers" emblazoned across your T-shirt?'

'You said on the phone he'd drowned.'

'I never said that nothing had been done to him before he'd drowned. What if his murderer had taken him by the throat until he was unconscious, and then thrown him in the water. Your T-shirt would have been the height of bad taste, then, wouldn't it?'

'Yes, sir. Sorry, sir.'

'Good night, Carmichael.'

'Good night, sir.'

'And bear in mind what I've said.'

'Yes, sir.' Carmichael was bloodied but unbowed, and he smiled as he fingered the scrap of paper in the pocket of his shorts with the all-important signature. Kerry would be over the moon when he showed it to her.

Chapter Nine

Saturday
Market Darley

Falconer's first task was sending off a forensic team to see what was to be found at the cordoned off part of the river where Bailey Radcliffe's earthly remains had been man-handled ashore.

He also took a phone call from Detective Constable Chris Roberts, still off sick with mumps. 'Sorry to bother you, gu ... sir.' He'd stopped himself in the nick of time from referring to his senior officer as 'guv'. 'I'm still feeling rather rough, but I've got to the point where things aren't as bad as they were, and, to be quite frank, I'm bored out of my mind.'

'I can understand that.' Roberts was a young man who lived on his own like Falconer, but was a good deal more social in his habits. Falconer thought briefly. If the man wasn't standing – slouching – in front of him looking mutinous, he found he didn't annoy him so much.

'I'll tell you what, when I've got all the notes together, I'll get one of the patrol cars to drop you off a copy of the file. Sometimes not being so involved helps people to see things more clearly and, if you come up with any brilliant theories or suggestions, just give me a ring.'

'That's brilliant, g ... sir.' He'd really have to be careful, he thought, remembering how Falconer had flown off the handle before when he was addressed as 'guv'. 'I'm desperate for something to take my mind off my swellings and getting my teeth into something totally unconnected will distract me from what's wrong with me.'

'Still need that wheelbarrow?' asked Falconer, in an attempt at humour.

'I think I could manage with a carrier bag now, sir. And it won't be long before I stop being infectious and can come back to work.'

'Good.' Maybe the boredom he was experiencing would make him more appreciative of having plenty to occupy him in his job.

'When shall I expect the file then, sir?'

'Sometime later today, when all the reports from forensics are written up, and I can get Carmichael to find the time to copy everything for you.'

'You're a diamond, sir.'

'Er, thanks, I think.'

Carmichael arrived as the inspector ended the call, still looking inordinately pleased with his snatching of the opportunity of getting his current hero's autograph, the evening before.

'You do realise we'll have to re-interview everyone we spoke to yesterday, don't you, Sergeant.'

'Why?'

'Because between us speaking to them and now, there's been a murder.'

'That's an awful lot of interviewing we've got to do.'

'It is, but it looks like we can discount the crew from *Chadwick's Chatterers* now, as they weren't anywhere near Fairmile Green last night.'

'Providing it's the same person, sir.'

'Whatever do you mean by that, Carmichael?'

'Providing that the person who murdered Bailey Radcliffe was the same person who was making attempts on Chadwick McMurrough's life.'

'Great! I had it all straight in my mind, and there you go, complicating everything. That's fair enough. We don't have any proof that it was the same person, so we'll have to treat them as two separate cases until we believe otherwise. Damn your eyes.'

'Sorry, sir, but you wouldn't want old Jelly on your back telling you that you hadn't considered all the possibilities.'

'No I would not. The man's practically a psychopath, and everything I do seems to enrage him. Well spotted, Carmichael. I'll make sure they've got separate case numbers.

'I think I'll just give Doc Christmas a ring. Sometimes he stays up into the early hours to do a post-mortem, other times he rises at 'sparrow fart', to get one out of the way. He's very keen on this aspect of his work.'

'Which is more than I am,' replied Carmichael, who found the cutting up of what had once been a person very upsetting indeed, both mentally and physically. He had been known to leave the scene of a post-mortem before now, just to find somewhere convenient to be sick; and to suffer nightmares afterwards. 'Thank God he didn't ask us to go to this one. I had a particularly good and solid breakfast this morning, and I don't fancy a rebate.'

Doc Christmas had, indeed, finished the post-mortem, and confirmed that Bailey Radcliffe had been hit on the back of the head with a blunt instrument before being introduced to the waters of the Little Darle to drown.

'His stomach contents showed what I expected; a fairly light meal taken about two-and-a-half hours before, and approximately three-quarters of a pint of lager and the remains of a packet of crisps – no suspicious substances –

all as anticipated.

'There was water in the lungs, consistent with samples of the Little Darle taken at the scene. There were no fibres or anything to help us identify the weapon, but it left an oval imprint – about an inch and a quarter across, in "old money" – just the one. It doesn't seem much to knock a man out, but Mr Radcliffe had quite a thin skull, and it did more damage than I would have anticipated.'

'Any idea what it could have been, or what it was made of?'

'No idea at all what it might have been, but at a guess, I'd say it was made of metal, for something of that small diameter to have knocked a full-grown man unconscious – even one without the thickest skull in the world.'

'Great! Where do we start?'

The doctor responded by singing the first few lines of a particular ditty made famous by Julie Andrews – well, he was a great fan of *The Sound of Music*.

'Very funny. I'll have to get a forensic team to start with the shed, outhouses, and garages, then move on to vehicles and houses – if the budget can stand the cost of such a thorough search. We need to get the number of suspects down first, though, otherwise it'll take them weeks. Those two had made enough enemies to be impressive.'

'Good luck, Harry. I'm glad I just had to fillet the body. Your job's much more complicated than mine.'

'You can say that again.'

Fairmile Green

Just after lunch Falconer and Carmichael headed back towards the crime scene, having decided to try to interview those that they had not been able to speak to the day before. They could try the ones they had already had a word with afterwards, just to get up to date, as it were.

The pub landlord would also need to be interviewed, for his account of what had happened in the pub yesterday evening, in case there was a clue there as to who had attacked and killed Bailey Radcliffe. Then they'd have to have another word with Chadwick McMurrough now he'd had a chance to absorb the events of the night before, and how they affected him.

They decided to start their marathon at Glass House, to get the bereaved out of the way first. Having parked right outside, they rang the doorbell, only for it to be opened by an almost unrecognisable Chadwick.

Instead of the flowing kaftan and the ridiculous trousers of the previous evening, he was wearing some very smart chinos and a black silk shirt, and his hair was dyed a Scandinavian blond, and set up in spikes rather than gelled into almost a helmet as it had been before.

A pine table in the kitchen was just visible as being set for two, and, as Falconer's eyesight and sense of smell were both excellent, there was both smoked salmon and caviar on it – these appeared to be common foodstuffs in this household. Dipsy was pawing at the closed sheet of glass which separated him from such luxuries, having been banned to the outside of the house for the duration of lunch and, in the sitting room, could be seen the outline of another person.

'Do come in, gents,' Chadwick bade them. 'And please excuse the mess in there. Bailey was going through his flies – fishing flies, that is – and he never put them away before we went out last night. You remember Robin Eastwood from last night? I'm just treating him to a little lunch to thank him for all his support after my tragic loss.'

'Very kind of you,' murmured the young man already seated in an armchair, looking very much at home.

'The least I could do, dearie,' replied Chadwick automatically, using his hands to indicate seats for the two detectives. 'Do sit yourselves down, and ask whatever it is you need to ask. Don't mind Robin,' and, for some unknown reason, frowned at his guest.

'No, it's all right. I'll take a walk round the garden while you're otherwise occupied.'

'Well, mind those bloody peacocks. Apparently there'll be someone coming over to pick them up on Monday. I don't know who, because Bailey wrote down the arrangements in the desk diary, and I simply could never read his handwriting. The man should have been a doctor, his scrawl was so illegible.'

'You seem to have recovered from your loss with remarkable speed, if you don't mind me saying so, Mr McMurrough,' declared Falconer, in disbelief at this almost light-hearted attitude.

'Oh, hadn't you heard? We gays are awfully shallow; incapable of real feelings, you know. In fact, many people say that I have hidden shallows rather than hidden depths.' Although Chadwick said this with a smile, it was a particularly world-weary one for one so young as he.

'I'm putting a brave face on things, Inspector. I have a show to record tonight, and I need to be in complete control of my emotions to be able to do that.'

'Of course,' mumbled Falconer apologetically. 'I'm sorry. I didn't think.'

When they were all settled and Carmichael had his notebook and pen at the ready, Falconer began with, 'Can you tell me who was in the pub last night? Then we'll move on to any personal enemies that Mr Radcliffe may have had.'

'I'll start with the second part first. Bailey got on with everyone. He was a very sociable and even-tempered creature, and the only person I know who had a personal grievance against him was Darren Worsley, his ex. As an afterthought, maybe you ought to include my ex in there, too. If I'd stayed with him and not been tempted to stray, Bailey and Darren might've still been together; although I doubt it, considering how much Darren had begun to drink.

'Also, on further thought, there would also be anyone from the vicinity of our garden, which does stretch right behind all the other houses along here, because of the peacocks – or, going back even further, because of all the disruption of the building works we needed to have done before we could move in.

'I suppose, on reflection, there must be quite a few round here who hold grudges against us for disturbing their peace. Both of us got endlessly button-holed during the barbecue, by people wanting to complain about something or other.'

Carmichael was scribbling away furiously in his usual mixture of genuine shorthand, and his own idiosyncratic abbreviations. It had taken a long time, but Falconer had almost got the hang of reading his sergeant's notes. It would be some time, however, before he was fluent, and he could extract only about sixty per cent of what was written in the man's notebook.

'And at the pub?' Falconer prompted the new 'suicide blonde'.

'Please excuse me if I start to put these fly boxes away. They're driving me mad, sitting all over the place making the room look untidy. I can talk while I do it.

'As expected, I got the usual bunch of fans around me to keep the attention where it should be – on me.' At this, he shot them a rather lame smile. 'There were a few locals in whom I hadn't met. Who else? Let me see. Oh, yes. Fairly early on, Gareth Jones put his head in, hoping for a quiet drink on his way home from work, but he saw me

130

and launched himself into a first-class hissy fit. Must still hanker after me, I suppose.

'I can't positively identify anyone else, I don't think. Hang on, there was that bloke that turned up at the party with his wife and kids, then went off with them in a huge huff just a few minutes later. I can't remember his name, though. And, of course, Robin looked in for a half not long before closing time.'

'I see your memory's coming back to you,' said Falconer drily.

'It's amazing, isn't it? If I remember anyone else, I'll give you a ring, but could I have another card, please. Your last one was in Bailey's pocket and, for obvious reasons, I don't have it any more.'

'Could you tell Mr Eastwood when he comes in that we'll be calling on him sometime this afternoon? If he has any other plans, perhaps he could consult your card and give me a ring on my mobile, so that we can arrange a more convenient time.'

'Surely you could talk to him here and now,' countered Chadwick, looking puzzled.

'It would be better in private, sir, if you don't mind.'

'Nothing to do with me, Inspector. I'll see you out.'

Once outside again, Carmichael turned to Falconer and said, 'He does seem to have got over it very quickly, doesn't he?'

'Dammit! I should have asked if the property was in joint names, or whether it was just in his. If both their names were on the deeds, that gives someone else outside the household a motive. After all, his share must go to someone, although I suppose it could go to McMurrough.'

'They haven't been an item that long, sir. He may not have had the opportunity to change his will. That might mean that his previous partner may have been left his share of the house.'

131

'Damn! That's another suspect for us to find and add to our ever-growing list.' Falconer's mood had already started to deteriorate since they had arrived in the village. 'And what's all this with the blonde spiky hair?'

'Maybe it's his idea of a new start, sir – a sort of clean slate.'

'Well, it didn't take him long to wipe the old one clean, did it? I fancy a change of scenery. Let's leave the places down here till last, and start down Old Darley Passage – blast – I hope that Worsley's sobered up. I meant us to get back to him this morning. No matter, if he's drunk again, or still drunk, I'm going to take him in and put him in a cell until he's fit to talk to us.

'We can finish off the first half of our interviews at the pub, then come back down here to finish off.' Falconer had decided that that was how it would be, and if it cheered him up a bit, Carmichael was happy to go along with it.

They called first, as they had done the previous day, at the house with the '2B' sign, but this time the door was opened to them by a young man with red curly hair and very freckled skin. 'Mr Westbrook?' enquired Falconer.

'Correct, but do call me Dean,' replied the householder. 'Do come in,' he invited, as they displayed their warrant cards. 'This must be about what happened last night. I heard about it on the local news at breakfast time.'

'Quite correct, Mr … Dean.'

They were ushered into a fairly small sitting room, rather overcrowded with a three-piece suite and a dining table and chairs, quite similar in size to the one in the Catcheside house, although the colours were nowhere near so hectic.

'I did meet the man, but only the once, at their barbecue party the other evening,' Dean offered.

'Did you also meet his partner, Chadwick McMurrough, your local celebrity,' asked Falconer with a twinkle in his eye at this sarcasm.

Dean's face suddenly fell, and his eyes began to swivel from side to side. 'I'm afraid I've known him for some considerable time,' he replied, with a catch in his voice.

'How come?' asked the inspector, immediately intrigued.

'We went to school together.'

'That must have been nice for you.'

'I think not.'

'Why's that?'

'He was a bully; a really persistent bully, and he made my life a misery for years.'

'Why?'

'Because he could. Basically he picked on anything that wasn't in line with what he saw as normal – hah! That's a laugh, considering how "un-mainstream" he is, now he's out of the closet and flaunting his sexuality on television to the great British viewing public. He picked on me because of my red hair and freckles.

'He must've called me every name under the sun, with "ginger" tacked on the end. And he wasn't just a mental bully either – he was a physical one, too. Chinese burns were his favourite torture. I suppose they didn't take a lot of effort for the enduring pain they produced.'

'Yet you went along to the party?' Falconer was surprised, not only at the amount of trepidation even the thought of the other man produced, but at the fact that this one had plucked up the courage to attend their house-warming gathering.

'I felt I might get the opportunity to talk to him man to man, and get rid of my phobia about him.'

'And, did you?'

133

'I lost my nerve. I didn't stay long at all; just long enough for one drink, then I slunk off into the night like a kicked puppy.'

'And where were you last night, between the hours of ten and eleven o'clock?'

'I was here, watching television.'

'Can anyone confirm that?'

'I'm afraid not. I don't have a girlfriend at the moment, and there were no phone calls or visitors to verify that.'

'We might need to speak to you again, Mr Westbrook,' announced Falconer, gone formal again. 'Thank you for your time.'

At Or Not 2B Gareth Jones was also at home to unscheduled callers. 'You're lucky to find me in,' he told them. 'I'm not long home – worked all morning on a rush job, and didn't get back here until nearly two.'

Carmichael gave Falconer an old-fashioned look about his previous regret at not getting to the village earlier. This time he took the lead. 'Perhaps we could come in and have a word with you about the unfortunate death of Mr Bailey Radcliffe.'

'Certainly. Tragic, that. I only saw him last night.'

'And how did that come about?' It was still Carmichael in the driving seat.

'On my way home from work. I thought I could just do with a pint or two after the long week I'd had, with Saturday morning still to come, but when I went into the pub, the first thing I saw was Chadwick with Radcliffe.'

'Did you speak to them, sir?'

'Not what you'd call a conversation. I made a few comments that weren't exactly complimentary, then the landlord asked me if I'd mind shutting my gob and getting out of his pub. I, of course, was only too glad to oblige.

Better a couple of beers here, in the comfort of my own home, than a drink there, with those two, rubbing my face in what they'd done to me, turning my life upside down like that.'

'You mean your break-up with Mr McMurrough?'

'That's right. I know he's a bit of a mincing nancy, and I don't look, at first glance, to be a poof, but we're the same under the skin. We were together for nearly a year, all through his time on *The Glass House*, then he got this two-week contract for a bit part in *Cockneys*, and suddenly he got all cagey, staying out late after rehearsal and filming.

The next thing I know, he's dumping me, and expecting me to find somewhere else to live. It's lucky this place was available immediately, otherwise I'd have been on the street. My parents haven't spoken to me since they found out which side I batted for, and my sister hasn't got room for me to stay with her. Luckily, he stumped up the deposit, or I wouldn't even have got this.'

'So, he really did turn your life upside down. It must have been a bit difficult to swallow.' Carmichael could really have been a little more careful with his wording, given the circumstances, Falconer thought with an uncomfortable smile.

'Look, I'm resilient, and I still had my work. All it meant was that I had to have a few business cards reprinted.'

'What exactly do you do?' Here, Falconer spoke for the first time.

'I'm self-employed; an electrician, so if you ever need any work done – no job too small – give me a tinkle. I'll give you my card.'

It was now Falconer's turn to give Carmichael one of his old-fashioned looks, which said 'now that's a very interesting piece of information, that is'.

'But he deprived you of a rather moneyed and pampered future, didn't he?' Falconer wasn't going to let go that easily.

'Oh, I've got my insurance. I've got loads of photographs, and even some recordings I did with my little cassette recorder, and bits of video on my smartphone. If I go to the press – which I will, when I'm ready – then I can really cash in. And his time in the public eye won't last long. That sort of star fades quite quickly, in my opinion.'

'But he's got his own chat show, now.'

'Yes. I must admit, I didn't expect that to happen.'

When they were outside once more, Falconer sighed and said, 'Well, that gets us exactly nowhere. Either of those two could have done it if it's a case of mistaken identity. They've both got an axe to grind, as far as Chadwick McMurrough goes, and Jones is actually an electrician.'

When Darren Worsley opened the door to their ring, he was, once again, holding on to it for support. 'Oh, it'sh you two again. Would you like a li'l drinky-poos, seeing ash it'sh the weekend?'

'That's quite all right, Mr Worsley. I don't think we'll come in today. I am, however, going to send one of my uniformed officers round to take you for a little ride. Is that all right?'

'Lovely. Ocifer. Li'l outing on a Sat'day. Jus' the ticket.'

'Goodbye then, for now.'

As he closed the door on them, Falconer made a quick call to the station, ascertained that PC Green was out on patrol, and asked for him to be directed to Worsley's address, to take him in as one of Her Majesty's temporary guests.

A few hours cooling his heels in a cell should sober him up nicely. Then they could interview him with a guarantee of a little more success than they'd had the day before.

Chapter Ten

Fairmile Green

Almost from force of habit, they found themselves outside Glass House, and decided that they might as well get their call over there first, as they knew Chadwick McMurrough had a rescheduled recording tonight and might even be already out. They needed to ask him about Bailey's will and who actually owned the house.

They'd had every intention of calling in at The Goat and Compasses before visiting this end of the village again but, somehow, the idea of a drink at the end of their last interview of the day proved more enticing than a coffee in the middle of the interviews, and so had headed south towards the property where they had made so many calls recently.

They were lucky in that McMurrough hadn't yet left, but Eastwood had, and he invited them in. He still didn't seem too heartbroken, but then he would have had to psych himself up for the delayed recording of his chat show later, and it was not surprising that he had worked hard to stay calm. He must be well on his way to being a professional by now.

'Go on in, and I'll put some coffee on,' he suggested, waving them into the living room, as he headed for the kitchen.

Falconer immediately sat down in one of the plumpfy

feather-stuffed armchairs, but Carmichael was more restless, and wandered around in a desultory way. He was over by the desk when he suddenly stopped and acted rather like a pointer dog, riveted by something that he must have seen on the desk top.

'Sir,' he hissed urgently. 'Over here. I don't want to touch it or move it.'

With a rolling of his eyes, Falconer struggled to his feet out of his enfolding nest, and wandered over towards his sergeant. 'Look at this, sir,' whispered Carmichael, pointing at a letter that was sitting, face up, beside the lap top.

It was a letter from the company responsible for the soap *Allerton Farm*, confirming a telephone conversation with Chadwick the day before, and offering him an appointment with their head of casting.

Both of them realised the importance of never having seen this piece of correspondence, and just had time to throw themselves down into chairs before Chadwick returned bearing a laden tray.

'I was a bit weird last night,' he said, without preamble. 'It was the shock, but I've had time to think since, and the only person I can think of who might have had it in for Bailey was Darren Worsley. And sorry I had Robin here earlier.'

Returning to the subject of Darren Worsley, he said, 'Those two had even bought a house together, you know. When Bailey left, he put the property on the market and, even though it was in only his name, he shared the proceeds with Darren: said it was the least he could do after making him homeless.'

'And did you buy this house together?'

'No. I paid for this, so I had something to show, if my career went pear-shaped.'

'And do you know how Mr Radcliffe left his assets?

Had he made a will?'

'I don't really know. I'll have to go through his stuff to see if I can find one. If not, I'll give his solicitor a tinkle to see what's what.'

He had already poured the coffee, and now handed them their cups, indicating that they should help themselves to milk and sugar.

'That idiot didn't even recognise the opportunity he had to put down a deposit on somewhere else,' he continued, returning to Worsley again with scarcely a break. 'From what I've heard on the grapevine, he's just drunk all the money away, living his life in a sea of self-pity, making up grandiose plans about what they would've done with their lives if I hadn't come along and stolen Bailey from right under his nose.

'Load of codswallop. He was already a lush. He hadn't worked since just after they moved into the house, and he started drinking in the mornings and was already half-cut when Bailey got home from work. He had no ambition beyond living off someone else's success, and Bailey is really – *was* really good at his job.'

Here he stopped, as Carmichael finished loading sugar into his cup. 'So you really do always take that much sugar?' he asked, remembering the last drink the sergeant had taken in the house, and looking horrified.

Carmichael nodded, sipping at the hot beverage.

'However do you taste the coffee?' Chadwick asked.

'Oh, I manage,' replied Carmichael good-naturedly, before returning to the notebook he had got out of his pocket as Chadwick was pouring the drinks.

'God, I still can't believe he's gone. I'm sorry, but I just can't afford to get upset today. If you want to talk about Bailey in any depth, I'm afraid you'll have to come back tomorrow. I'm not being difficult, honestly. I just have a responsibility to the studio and production crew to

140

turn up fit for work.'

Although he had expressed surprise at Carmichael's sweet tooth, his speech was almost as if it was on automatic pilot, and he seemed a bit distracted. He had, however, had his partner murdered the previous evening, so it was hardly surprising that he couldn't concentrate very well.

Realising that this was all they were going to get, Falconer waited for Carmichael to stop his scribbling, then they drained their cups to the dregs and stood to leave. 'Thank you for your time, sir. We really appreciate it, and will be calling on you again. If you think of anything else, please don't hesitate to give us a ring.'

'Please catch whoever did this. I thought I'd have done anything for publicity, but this is just a step too far,' he said as he saw them out.

Once outside again, they decided to start where they had the day before, and turned their steps towards Woodbine Cottage. 'What did you make of that letter, sir?'

'It looks to me like he's looking to further his career beyond a chat show. Trying to get into a soap is as good a way as any to get started in the acting trade, and he has been in *Cockneys*. Even if it won't lead to the Royal Shakespeare Company, there'll always be a part in panto waiting for him, and as many supermarket openings as you could shake a stick at. He'll not go short if he takes that route.'

'Suppose so. He doesn't strike me as someone who would want to get into serious acting.'

'Hardly. He's more the outrageous sort. I don't think the *Farm*'s had a queen yet. He should be like a breath of fresh air blowing through the beautiful countryside up north.' Falconer was already convinced, and thought that the head of casting on *Allerton Farm* would be too. It was too good and too current an opportunity to miss.

What they assumed to be Mrs Fairchild opened the door of Woodbine Cottage to them today, checked their credentials and asked them in with a little moue of distaste, as she said, 'I suppose it's about the death of *him* down the road – not that he's any loss to anyone except that other freak that lived with him.'

'I presume you're referring to the murder of Mr Radcliffe from Glass House,' said Falconer, in a cold tone. He had not looked forward to returning here, after meeting this woman's son the day before.

'I never even spoke to him,' she continued, eventually pointing to a man in a chair by the fireplace. 'This is my Roger. He and I don't hold with all that unnatural stuff. Against nature it is.'

'An abomination before the Lord,' chipped in Roger.

'Are you religious people?' asked the inspector.

'Not so as you'd notice, but we know what's right and what's wrong.'

'And something that was wrong, as far as we were concerned, was that mincing queen McMurrough winning *The Glass House*.'

'Your son was in that, wasn't he?' asked Carmichael, just for something to say.

'That's right,' confirmed Mr Fairchild. 'Did you see him?'

'No, we talked to your son yesterday,' replied Falconer, just to straighten matters out. He didn't want to get embroiled in deep discussions about a puerile television reality show which he had never seen, and in which he had no interest whatsoever.

'You've spoken to Rufus?'

'Briefly. Yes.'

'He never said nothing. RUFUS!'

She yelled this last at the top of her voice, and there came the sound of footsteps thundering down the stairs, a call of 'I've got a college workshop,' before the front door slammed, and the sound of a moped disappearing in the direction of Market Darley could be heard.

'Little sod never said a word about you coming here yesterday,' commented his father, trying without much success to light an evil-smelling old pipe.

'He's doing a drama course at college, you know,' put in the little sod's mother, a proud smile now decorating her chops, but her countenance darkened again as she added, 'He should've won that show, you know.

'I reckon that young pervert must've had something on someone in the production crew, and been blackmailing whoever was responsible for spinning the editing, making it in his favour, and against our Rufus.'

'We spoke to that McMurrough freak at their so-called party – briefly,' contributed Roger, once more re-joining the conversation, now that his pipe was puffing out plumes of vile-smelling smoke.

'But he just insulted us and walked off. We went off and had a good old moan with Nerys and Vince – them from two doors away,' Rita informed them, as they both started coughing.

'So you never actually spoke to Mr Radcliffe?'

'That we did not!' declared Mr Fairchild, with a flourish of the stem of his pipe to emphasise his negative statement.

'Then we'll be off and leave you in peace. We'll see ourselves out,' Falconer assured them, adding under his breath to Carmichael, 'Before we choke on that foul smoke and the even fouler atmosphere of hatred.'

'What a delightful couple,' declared Falconer, as they walked to the house next door, 'Not.'

'Shows just how far our society hasn't come in

accepting people that just don't fit the usual mould. Thank God they weren't Caribbean, or they'd probably have fire-bombed the house.'

'It would've been a lot less trouble for us,' judged Falconer, drily and selfishly.

'You don't mean that, sir.'

'Of course I don't. The only thing I really can't stand, though, is bigots. I feel dirtied, as if I need a damned good scrub down in the shower.'

'Ditto, sir.'

So far they had both had an open mind over the Innocents, having not yet met them, and having forgotten what had happened to their cat.

Anthea Innocent opened the door to them and, when she found out who they were, went right off the deep end. 'He ran right over poor Cuddles' body – completely squashed her – killed her instantly, and now *he's* dead, and never punished – I suppose there's nothing you can do about it. Animals simply don't have rights in today's society.'

'Calm down, Mrs Innocent,' Falconer soothed, as a man came into the hall right behind her and put his arm round her waist.

'Now, don't you go upsetting yourself all over again, Anthea,' he said. 'We'll get straight back on the horse and get a cute little kitten. We'll find one somewhere, and you can have another little sweetie to dote on. Who are these gentlemen? We don't buy at the door, you know. There's a sign on the gate.'

'We're the police, Mr Innocent; here about Mr Radcliffe's death.'

'Never even met him, we haven't, but if I had've done, I'd have busted his nose for him, running over our poor little cat like that, not looking where he was going.'

'Did neither of you meet either of the men at Glass House?' asked the inspector, still reeling at the venom that had emanated from this young woman, whose face had grown red with her rising temper.

'No.' they replied, in unison.

'We'll be on our way, then. Thank you for your time,' said Falconer, swivelling quickly a hundred and eighty degrees, and marching towards the front gate, Carmichael right on his heels, as anxious as him to get away from such a young harridan.

Neither Nerys nor Vince Catcheside was out at work today, and they were invited into a bleak sitting room in which there was no air; no window or door left open, and the strong smell of dog was discernible, easily traceable to a very elderly and none-too-clean spaniel in a basket in the corner of the room.

'You here about those two homosexuals, are you, or just the one who got himself topped?' asked the very unlovely Vince.

'Whoever did that, did this village a favour.' Nerys put in her two-penn'orth in a most unsavoury manner.

'So you weren't friends with them, then?' Might as well put the cat among the pigeons. If it was going to be uncomfortable for them, he might as well make it uncomfortable for these two, too, thought the inspector.

'No bloody way, mate: not with the likes of them. We wouldn't risk it, in case we caught something. Never know what they've got, that sort. Could be carrying all sorts of diseases not visible to the naked eye.'

'But you were quite happy to attend their barbecue?'

'That was different. We wanted a nose at what they'd done with the old place after all that disruption. And there wasn't any harm in drinking their booze. Alcohol sterilizes things. As for the food, if it was barbecued, any germs would have been killed by the heat.'

It almost made sense. 'But you didn't know them?'

'Absolutely not. Wouldn't mix with their kind if you paid me.'

'But you went to their party?' If that wasn't mixing with them, Falconer was a monkey's uncle.

'That was different.'

They left after that, before either of them could get into a homophobic rant. If that had happened, both of them felt they would have needed restraining from giving the Catchesides a damned good thumping.

Falconer winced as he heard the shouting and yelling coming from the inside of the next house, as Carmichael put his finger to the doorbell of Myrtle Cottage.

This time it was a sour-faced Mr Warren who answered their ring, and he just inclined his head to his rear to bid them enter. The living room was utter pandemonium, with the three ambient children throwing whatever they could lay their hands on at each other, even the baby trying to join in from its position on the floor, while Mrs Warren ran round between the four of them to try to disarm them.

'Bit lively today, aren't they?' commented Carmichael, as a metal toy car whizzed past his ear. It looked like he and the inspector had become the new target for the little devils.

Falconer ducked as a small doll flew over his head, thus failing to dodge the plastic dog that hit him on the head, as he straightened up again.

'Nothing's changed since yesterday. You can talk to Christopher if you like, because he was at work when you came before – isn't that where he always is – but I've got nothing to add. I was in here all last night with a baby who wouldn't sleep no matter what I tried.'

After his wife's bitter comment about his regular absence from the fray, the sour expression on Mr Warren's face deepened, and he motioned towards the comparative sanctuary of a tiny dining room, where it was marginally quieter.

'I hadn't even tried to get to know them,' he told them, as soon as they had all taken a seat round the table, seeing this as the only way that four people could be comfortably accommodated within its space-limiting walls.

'I don't know any of the neighbours – only to say hello to. She's right; I am always at work – I have a very demanding job, that often dictates that I do overtime.'

'But you went to their house-warming barbecue?' asked Carmichael.

'We were only there a few minutes when someone chastised the kids, and she was off, in high dudgeon, and I had to follow to show solidarity. Actually, I think our kids are a bunch of destructive little hooligans, and it didn't bother me if someone else wanted to try to instil a little discipline into them, but they wrap her round their little finger, and make me glad I don't have to spend too much time here with them.

'And I got sent back later to relay madam's complaints about how the noise made things worse with the kids, and how their ruddy peacocks kept us all awake at night. That was fun, I can tell you.'

'That's very honest of you, sir,' Falconer thanked him, while thanking God that he lived on his own, and didn't have to deal with this sort of disruption in his spare time. He'd go stark raving mad in no time at all if his home life resembled this poor soul's, and he mentally wished him luck with picking up some more overtime.

This was the point where they passed Glass House to visit the three houses on the other side of it and the one in

Market Street. The first property was Riverbanks, where they had chatted with Gerald and Lucille Sutherland yesterday, and shouldn't take very long, as they had made their position perfectly clear at this first meeting.

As they had expected, neither of them admitted having been out in the village the evening before. In fact, they had gone over to Market Darley to visit friends, which was easy to check up on, and had not returned until nearly midnight, when all the fuss was over.

It had only been when Gerald went out for a newspaper that morning that they had learnt the news of their neighbour's death. Taking the telephone number of the friends they had visited the night before, the two detectives went on their way, calling at Green Gates next.

Mr Oliver Smallwood had returned from his business trip the evening before about seven o'clock, and was now available to speak to them, but he was as devoid of information as everyone else had been. It was his wife Ellie who had gone round about their Darling, as he had not been there, and he'd not spoken to either of them since they had moved in.

'I had thought of going round to complain about the noise nuisance from their mad birds – not at all suitable for a garden where there are near neighbours, don't you think? But, I could never be bothered. There was always something else to do; paperwork, you know, and we do have a social life.

'It's Ellie that's had to put up with more than me, although I did object to the disruption when I was here at weekends, but she can cope with it better than I can, being so wrapped up with her plans to breed Shih Tzus – and eventually win Best of Breed, even a Best in Show at Crufts, sometime in the dim and distant future.

'Me? I'll just be happy if she makes enough to cover the salary she's given up, and helps me balance the books on this place and retain our present lifestyle. I'd be grateful if they – *he*'d – get rid of those birds, though.'

'I think that'll happen, sir, and in the not too distant future.'

At River View, Robin Eastwood took a little rousing, as the weather was fair again and, back at home once more, was at his ease in a sun lounger in the back garden. When he finally answered the door, he was all flashing eyes, teeth, and smiles.

'Do come on in. I'll get a couple of folding chairs and we can talk outside in the garden. Just give me a minute or two to put together a tray of cold drinks and I'll be with you.'

'Sociable soul, isn't he?' commented Falconer, as they strolled outside on to the lawn.

'His sort usually are,' replied Carmichael cryptically. 'I thought you'd have noticed by now.'

'What the hell are you babbling about, Sergeant?'

'He's one of them, isn't he?'

'Is he? One of what?' Falconer really had no idea what Carmichael was babbling about.

'He's gay.'

'He's never!'

'Oh yes, he is. He set off my "gay-dar" as soon as I met him yesterday evening. I thought you'd have noticed too, sir.'

'Nothing was further from my mind. I thought he'd just popped round to support McMurrough?'

'As if. He smelt fresh meat, and was in there as fast as he could get. McMurrough's quite a catch, you know, even without the lure of a possible part in *Allerton Farm*.'

'Never! How mercenary!'

'Yes, sir. Here he comes with a couple of chairs now.'

It was lucky Eastwood had to go back into the house to load his tray of refreshments, because Falconer was too stunned to speak.

The resultant interview was curt, and lasted only long enough for a glass of chilled lemonade to be consumed. In fact, Falconer nearly choked, trying to drink his so fast, and nearly did so again when Eastwood informed them he worked as a solicitor; a partner in a local firm.

Afterwards, as they headed towards the footbridge that would allow them to get to the pub, it was only Carmichael who was in a talkative mood. 'He admitted to going for a drink about ten o'clock, sir. He made no bones about being out and about in the village fairly late.'

There was no reply, so Carmichael felt obliged to carry out the conversation with himself. 'At least if he did that, he'd have a defence if anyone told us they'd seen him. Pretending to be at home all evening would have cut no mustard if he'd been spotted, so it only made sense to go for a drink, and McMurrough said he'd dropped in for a quick one before closing time.

'It would be easy for him to have hung around until McMurrough had seen Radcliffe off home, then get in there and do for him. And he had a motive, if he had his eye on young McMurrough for himself. There're much more of an age, after all. Radcliffe must have been – what? – twenty-five, thirty years older than his partner.'

They had stopped outside The Goat and Compasses, and Falconer finally spoke. 'I hear where you're coming from, and I believe you've made several valid points. We'll chew them over after we've done our stuff in here. Speaking for myself, I could murder a half, if not a full, pint.'

'Me too, sir,' agreed Carmichael. Neither of them drank much, and if they wanted more fluid, would probably order lemonade and lime.

The landlord of The Goat and Compasses was a big man called Terry Watkins. He had been at the pub eight years, and knew all his local customers by name, as well as their usual orders.

He remembered the night in question well because, apart from the murder, it was only the second one when McMurrough had spent time on the premises, this time gathering punters round him and keeping them there drinking for longer than they usually would have stayed.

'It was a good night for takings, in the end, after a very slow start, and I hope he comes in regularly – once he's got over his tragic loss, of course.' These last words were not spoken with any real empathy. The whole emphasis was on future profits.

He remembered well Gareth Jones arriving at the bar, and told them that he didn't put up with any nonsense on his premises, and had made it clear that Jones should have a beer at home, and the man had left without causing any further upset.

'I used to box a bit when I lived in London, and I don't tolerate any rough stuff in my pub. If necessary, I'm prepared to wade in myself and pull the buggers apart. I won't have it, and my regulars know it. This is a respectable drinking place.'

He also remembered Robin Eastwood coming in about ten o'clock for just the one, and confirmed that he had left just before closing time. 'He often does that. Says he likes a bit of fresh air before he goes to bed. It takes all sorts, doesn't it?'

He had no more to add, at that point, and felt he had been sufficiently helpful, finally gazing round his pub, full of old beams and horse-brasses with a smug smile. He ran a clean establishment, well-adorned with brass and copper;

the curtains were a suitably country chintz, and he was pleased with life in general, especially with the prospect of the current media darling becoming a regular.

Their thirsts quenched, the two detectives headed back to Market Darley and Darren Worsley, hopefully banged up in a cell and sobering up nicely.

Green had done his job, and they found the man in a cell that reeked of alcohol and stale sweat, but he was still far from sober. 'I demand a fag break!' he yelled into Falconer's face when they arrived at his place of incarceration. 'There's no bleeding smoking in here, and I need a fag. It's against my human rights to deprive me of one of those, so I demand that someone takes me somewhere where I can have a smoke. I am an addict, you know.'

'Carmichael – handcuffs. Then take Mr Worsley out into the back yard where the bicycle shed is, for his fix, then deposit him back here, and I'll see you in the office before we go home.'

Worsley was not slurring like he had earlier, but his speech was too careful to be normal, and his gait was still a little staggering. It was hardly worth trying to get any sense out of him until he was fully *compos mentis*. The morning would be timely enough.

They were getting nowhere fast, and Falconer would be glad of a bit of solid evidence, or a decent clue to the killer's identity. It was all very frustrating, not even having a prime suspect.

Chapter Eleven

Sunday
Market Darley

Although neither Falconer nor Carmichael were scheduled to work on the Sabbath, they had a duty to go into the station to question their detainee from the day before, damn his drunken eyes.

Bob Bryant, as usual, was on duty at the desk – when wasn't he? – and led them to Worsley's cell. 'He's been a bit lively since you went home last night, but he finally settled down and, when he had his breakfast brought to him this morning, it looked like he'd slept it off, and was finally sober, so I think you might be all right.'

'Good,' commented Carmichael, 'because the inspector's coming to mine for his Sunday dinner.'

Falconer smiled weakly, while Bob Bryant smirked, and merely said, 'That's nice.'

Worsley was found to be dozing on his mean bunk, his blanket pushed on to the floor, it being quite warm in the cells with their lack of windows and little ventilation.

'Good morning, Mr Worsley,' Falconer greeted the man, bringing him back to wakefulness. 'I'm sorry we had to detain you, but we are in the middle of a murder investigation, and it was important that we had a chance to speak to you when you were sober. I'm sure you

153

understand how important it is for us to follow up any clue, no matter how small.'

'I know I'm unbearable when I'm drunk, but I don't know whether I can be of any help to you, even sober, although I suppose there are always nuggets of information that could help you on your way,' said Worsley, for the first time since they had first met him, sounding rational.

Carmichael got out his notebook, and Falconer took a seat at the other end of the bunk.

'What do you remember of the last few days, Mr Worsley? Can you remember anything that happened on the night that Mr Radcliffe was murdered?'

Worsley's face fell, and Falconer apologised. 'I'm sorry, sir. I had momentarily forgotten that you two used to be partners, and that this must be painful for you.'

'It's all right. I'm fine most of the time, but then, most of the time I'm off my face, and can't really think about anything seriously.' He scratched at his uncombed hair and thought for a moment.

'We used to double-date, you know – just occasionally – Bailey and I and Chadwick and Gareth Jones. I suppose it was because those two were getting it together, and were desperate to spend more time with each other, but Gareth and I didn't even notice.'

'Where did you go as a foursome?

'It was usually to a club in some town or other; somewhere where there were lots of people, lots of noise, and lots of booze. That way they could get Gareth and me wasted, and disappear off into a dark little corner to spend some time alone.

'There are gay clubs out there, even round here, if you know where to look, and we're not unrealistically far from London – especially if you've got money to burn and can afford a taxi.'

'So you think they might have been cheating on the two of you even before both couples split up?' asked Carmichael, fascinated by this glimpse into a lifestyle about which he knew nothing.

'Oh, absolutely. We'd go back to ours, and they'd put the drunks to bed, then get it together downstairs while we two sots were unconscious.'

'Do you know this for certain, sir?'

'Not a hundred per cent, but let's say, if my suspicions were made of concrete, they'd nearly be set by now. You do know what Gareth's planning to do, don't you? I only wish I'd been sober enough to come up with the same idea before we split up, but I was always on the booze, even then.'

'What's that, sir?' asked Falconer, playing the innocent.

'He's been collecting little notes and messages, photographs and bits of video from his smartphone, ever since McMurrough went into *The Glass House*. He used to confide in me quite a lot, in the early days before, I suspect, those two got serious about each other.'

Originally he was only gathering material just for memories, but he got to thinking about what would happen if they ever split up – oh, yes, he considered the idea of where it would leave him if McMurrough hit the big time.

'And he was right, wasn't he? Anyway, by then, he had quite an archive of their time together – even recordings of tender moments between them, and he's planning to go to the press and sell his story.

'What with my poor ex – poor old bedazzled Bailey – getting the chop, what he's got will be hot news. He'll make a bundle, and might even get invited on to someone's chat show into the bargain – hopefully not McMurrough's!'

'You really think he's going to do it?'

'He's probably sorting his archive as we speak, and considering which tabloid would pay the most. It wouldn't surprise me if he put it up for auction between the lot of them. You know what they're like for a story like that.'

At that point, Bob Bryant entered the cell and said that Superintendent Chivers had made one of his surprise Sunday visits, and would like a word with Falconer.

Muttering brimstone and fire under his breath at this interruption, Falconer rose and apologised to Worsley for the hiatus in the interview, then told Carmichael to get off and find himself some coffee, and that he'd meet him back in the office before they returned to the cell.

Sitting smugly behind his desk at the thought of this bandit raid on the investigation, Chivers fixed Falconer with a beady eye, and asked, 'Well? Have you made an arrest yet? Worked out who did it? It's about time. I hear you've got someone in the cells. Is that our man?' He had arranged to do a press conference, and greedily anticipated having a suspect well in their sights before he appeared before the reporters and cameras. How he loved a bit of very public showing off.

'I don't think so, sir.'

'Why ever not?'

'I don't believe he was in any state at the time the victim was attacked.'

'Who exactly is this fellow in custody?'

'He's not exactly in custody – he's in for questioning. He's a habitual drunk. And I brought him in to sober him up so that I could question him properly. As to who he is, he's the ex-partner of the deceased.'

'Another bum boy, then. Just how many of them are there in this blasted village?' He knew he'd have to be a bit more nice-mouthed when he faced the mob, but he didn't see why he shouldn't be his normal prejudiced self inside his own office.

'I think that's rather less than politically correct, sir,' said Falconer, wincing slightly, as if he expected to be hit.

'I don't give a flying fig about what you think. If he's the ex-partner of the deceased, then you can arrest him. That's enough circumstantial evidence for me, if he doesn't have a watertight alibi. Does he?'

'No, sir, but he couldn't have done it ...'

'Couldn't have done it, my arse. Arrest the man and find the evidence later.'

'But ...'

'Do as I say, Inspector, or it'll be the worse for you and your career.'

Falconer left the office thinking that God was supposed to be in a good mood on Sundays, and feeling desperately uncomfortable about having to arrest Darren Worsley. He had a gut feeling that the man had had nothing to do with Radcliffe's demise, and he had been ordered to act against his better judgement.

They drove in their separate cars to Carmichael's house in Castle Farthing, and the inspector found that he was quite looking forward to having a meal cooked for him on a Sunday, and, oddly for him, the company, although this latter was just to take his mind off what he had just done at the station.

He could smell the cooking from outside, and was looking forward to greeting Kerry and his godchildren, when he suddenly found himself on his back on the floor, his face soaked, and his view obscured by a familiar muzzle, as he also became aware of two large paws planted firmly on his chest.

There was no way he could get up, and he was forced to lie there while Kerry informed them, 'Mr Moore dropped Mulligan off this morning, to give them more time to pack. I said you wouldn't mind.'

157

'That's fine. As I always say, the more the merrier,' replied Carmichael, tugging fruitlessly at the dog's collar.

Falconer squirmed beneath his canine burden, but could do nothing effective against such a bulk. 'Will someone get this brute off me?' he pleaded, quite winded from his fall.

The children had evidently arrived to observe the fun, and he heard Dean say, 'Look at Mulligan kissing Uncle Harry!'

'He loves you, Uncle Harry,' added Kyle, for good measure.

Carmichael gave another tug at the collar and came over all literary. 'I believe he's loving Uncle Harry "not wisely, but too well".'

'What does that mean, Daddy?'

'Will you get this brute off of me before I either drown or suffocate?'

'I'm doing my best, sir, but he's not being very co-operative.'

'He's crushing the life out of me.'

'Oh, leave him to me,' sounded Kerry's voice, wearily. 'Come on, Mulligan – cheese.'

The dog's ears pricked up, and he immediately bounded away to the source of this irresistible promise. He loved a bit of cheese, and had been able to recognise the word since he was a puppy – as in not *quite* so large.

As Mulligan slobbered at a small pile of grated cheese on the kitchen floor, Falconer's saviour added, 'That's all it takes. I always use cheese when I want his full and undivided attention. It works like magic.'

'I didn't know that,' said Carmichael.

'That's because you never pay attention or listen to what I say,' replied Kerry, with a superior tone. 'Come on, Inspector Falconer, let's get you cleaned up and sat down with a cup of tea in your hand. I can safely leave the food to its own devices for a while.'

With Mulligan calmed down and cheese on hand in case there were any further outbreaks of over-enthusiasm on the dog's part, they all enjoyed a very well-cooked Sunday roast, and Falconer felt himself really unwind for the first time since the beginning of the case.

The day passed very pleasantly, marred only by Mulligan's insistence on lying on Falconer's lap, where there was not enough room to accommodate the whole dog. The brute had also enjoyed the leftovers from their roast meal, and, occasionally – much too often for Falconer's liking – a pungent cloud arose from his back end and made his beloved choke on the fumes.

Mulligan eventually compromised on his position, with the inspector sat on one end of the sofa, with Mulligan's head in his lap, the rest of the besotted animal taking up all the space left on that particular piece of furniture.

It was only the tinkling of the inspector's mobile phone that finally roused the dog, for he didn't like the ringtone, and finally got down on the floor and settled in front of the fireplace.

It was such a relief not to be covered in the top half of the ever-so-slightly pungent heap of fur, and Falconer was very grateful, as his legs had been numb for hours, and it was nice to get the opportunity to massage some feeling back into these, hitherto useless, limbs. It was about eight o'clock and, at almost the same time, Carmichael's landline rang. One call was from Chivers, the other from Bob Bryant. There had been another murder in Fairmile Green.

Fairmile Green

This time they parked outside River View in Market

Street, which was the very smartly furnished and decorated residence of Robin Eastwood. The place was unrecognisable from their last visit there. They also took note of quite a pack of vehicles outside Glass House. The press were doing their best to be ready to catch any pearls of wisdom that dropped from their current young hero's lips.

River View, they found, had been thoroughly turned over. The furniture was overturned, drawers pulled out, cupboards ransacked, and there was paint sprayed in meaningless squiggles all over the walls and the expensive rugs which were scattered over the parquet floor. It was a very sorry sight that greeted them.

'Where's Eastwood?' asked Falconer, hardly able to believe that someone could do so much damage to what had been a beautiful room, although experience told him otherwise. Somehow, though, it was behaviour he thought of more in relation to the towns than the villages. This was fairly unusual, so far out in the sticks.

PC Merv Green was guarding the place while he waited for a SOCO team, and replied, 'He's in the bedroom. He must have been having an early night or something when this joker broke in.'

'At this time? More likely he was changing clothes or having a shower,' put in Carmichael, anxious to make a contribution.

'Well he obviously didn't disturb whoever it was, or his body would be down here. All this must have been done after he was killed. It looks like pure spite to me,' added Falconer. 'Let's get upstairs and see what's what.'

Eastwood was lying on the floor at the foot of the bed, with a large knife protruding from his abdominal area, a fair amount of blood on his body. He was buck naked.

'This is a pretty kettle of fish, isn't it? Who found the body?' Carmichael shrugged his shoulders, and the inspector called downstairs, 'Merv, who found him?'

'His business partner,' called back Green. 'He wanted to consult him about a client tomorrow, and he's a key-holder in case of emergency, so he let himself in, and found all this waiting for him. I had to let him go for family reasons, but I'm pretty positive he wasn't involved. His business is in the village, though, so he shouldn't be too difficult to track down.' Although this was unorthodox behaviour, Falconer let it go for now, praying that it wouldn't come back to bite them on the bum.

'Have we got fingerprints and photography people on their way? The usual mob?'

'A full team, sir.'

'What about Doc Christmas?'

'I can see him just pulling up outside, sir.' Green's voice was already getting hoarse with shouting.

'Send him straight up, will you, please?'

'Yes, sir.'

Christmas joined them within a couple of minutes, suitably dressed in his now-trendy forensic 'onesie', and gave them one of his Paddington stares. 'Are you starting one of your massacres again, Harry? You've done this to me before. Not content with one body, you feel you have to go on until you've got a full set. Rumour has it that you've started on the gay population now. Is this true? It's going to do nothing for our relations with the pink community.'

'Knock it off, Philip. That's simply not funny, although it is true that both victims have been homosexual; not that they knew each other, so I don't see that there's any connection.'

'OK, keep your hair on. And I couldn't even have said that at the last crime scene, or you'd have been down my throat before I could defend myself.'

161

'I'm sorry, Philip. I had a lousy morning, then I spent the day at my sergeant here's house, and had a thoroughly relaxing afternoon, then the phone rang, and all hell has been let loose. I didn't mean to get at you. It's just me feeling sorry for myself, as well as the poor bugger I had to arrest this morning, on some stupid whim of Jelly's.'

This being the widely used reference to Superintendent Chivers, Doc Christmas knew exactly who he meant. 'Has he got a bee in his bonnet again?'

'Yes, and he won't listen to reason. Anyway, it's a long story which I won't bore you with now. Take a look at this one and give me your professional opinion.'

'Pretty obvious isn't it, at first glance. He's been stabbed in the guts, and has died, probably from internal injuries, I'd say. No, no defence wounds on the hands, so he wasn't expecting an attack. It all looks pretty efficient to me, and you know I can't go any further than that until I've done the post mortem. He's not warm, though.'

'No? So you couldn't estimate time of death?'

'Not without further investigation. Sorry.'

'We'll take a last look around here then, and get back to the station. I'll await your report and the one from forensics when they've been over the place with a fine-toothed comb. Come on, Carmichael. I need another word with Green.'

What he needed from Green was the name and address of the professional partner who had discovered the body and the vandalism at the house. If he'd been here before, he might be able to tell them if there was anything missing.

He also needed the name of the next of kin so the body could be officially identified. If Eastwood's business partner couldn't say whether anything had been taken or not, the next of kin might be able to oblige.

As they left the house, Carmichael asked Falconer if he

still suspected the neighbours now there'd been another death. 'I just can't seem to see any connection between the two men, so it's very difficult to form any opinion just yet. We need more information before we can start formulating theories,' he replied in his usual, sensible, dry manner.

'No gut feelings? No hunches?'

'Completely out-of-stock in the gut feelings and hunches departments, I'm afraid.'

By the time they got back to the station to write up their notes, it would be too late to interview anyone tonight, but they could start straight away tomorrow with the man who had come across this horror, when he'd probably be in a calmer state than he was tonight, having had time overnight to let the shock wear off a little.

The last thing he'd do that night, Falconer decided, was to let Darren Worsley go home. Although it didn't look as if the two deaths were connected, he couldn't have been responsible for this second one, and he was absolutely sure that he'd had nothing to do with the first one, either. At least he could do one good deed today to try to offset his callous behaviour – albeit on orders – earlier on.

Chapter Twelve

Monday
Market Darley

The following morning, there was a preliminary report from the SOCO team, but there were test results to wait for from forensics so it, by its very nature, could not be a full report.

There was also an e-mail from Doc Christmas who, although he had not yet carried out the post mortem, had taken blood samples the previous evening – he was a workaholic, as his wife could testify – and discovered the presence of a sedative in the sample, as yet unidentified, but of interest. He intended to carry out the post mortem that morning, and would send his report as soon as he'd completed it.

'How very interesting. Do you see this, Carmichael? There was a sedative in Eastwood's blood stream. Even if he took sleeping tablets, I'd have thought it was a bit early to take them, so I'm suspicious that said sedative was not self-administered. It looks rather like he was drugged before he was killed.'

'That might account for the lack of defence wounds, too. Maybe he was too woozy to take in exactly the danger he was in,' added Carmichael.

Falconer looked thoughtful. 'It will be interesting to see if there are any fingerprints on the shaft of that knife. Well, best be off to see this Mr Dingwall. I rang him first thing, and he said he had to be in the office on time today as he had a client due.

'I've arranged for us to call on him at ten-thirty in his office, which happens to be in Fairmile Green rather than Market Darley, where he lives.'

'Whereabouts in the village?' asked the sergeant, not having noticed a solicitors' office on his previous visits there, although he had not been on the lookout for one, so it was hardly surprising, as such an establishment rarely boasts a garish and eye-catching frontage.

'It's in the High Street between the bakery and the craft shop,' replied Falconer, who had taken the trouble to ask Mr Dingwall, in the pursuit of saving them some time-wasting searching on both sides of the road.

'We can also call in on Mr McMurrough too, see if he's remembered anything that could be of use to us – provided there isn't too thick a crowd of media for us to wade our way through.'

'And to see where he was last evening.'

'We didn't even wait for time of death from the Doc, so I think we'd better wait until we're informed a little better before we narrow it down.'

'Why don't you give him a ring?' suggested the sergeant. 'We could do with that bit of information before we go out.'

'Of course we could. Whatever am I thinking of?' replied Falconer, colouring up with embarrassment at his own naïveté. Picking up the phone, he dialled Doc Christmas's number.

'Hello there, Harry. I was about to ring you myself. I was so excited at what I'd found in the dead man's blood that I didn't think to put in the strange thing about the time of death.'

'Strange thing? What's that?'

165

'He died in the morning. Somewhere between eight and twelve o'clock is all I can say at the moment. We all assumed he'd died in the evening because he was upstairs, but he didn't. He'd been lying there all day, so if you're asking anyone where they'd been at a certain time, it would be Sunday morning, not early evening.'

'That's a bit of a turn-up for the books, isn't it?'

'It is a bit. Oh, and the sedative was ketamine. I suppose you know it's used by vets to sedate horses, and in some hospitals, too, but it is also, for some inexplicable reason, used as a recreational drug by young people on a night out, now. God knows why. It doesn't make any sense, but then, what sense did what young people get up to ever make?'

'True. I hope this doesn't mean we're looking for a murderous veterinary surgeon.'

'More likely someone who can get their hands on it. I should try your local pushers. And don't try to tell me that Market Darley and its environs doesn't have anyone so vile and disgusting, because I simply won't believe you.'

'I'm so glad I phoned you. We're just on our way out, and the time of death is really relevant to the questioning.'

'You'll get a copy of my full report as soon as it's ready.'

'Thanks a million, Philip.' Putting the phone back into its cradle, Falconer turned to his sergeant and said, 'Well, that little bit of information certainly stopped us from getting egg all over our faces when we call on McMurrough.'

'I'd say, sir.'

Fairmile Green

They were able to park right outside the solicitors' office,

166

and Clive Dingwall's client had already left when they entered the premises of Dingwall and Eastwood, to be ushered through to the remaining partner's office by the receptionist.

Dingwall proved to be a man in his late thirties with a prematurely bald head, which he disguised by shaving off the rest of his hair to give a more uniform look. He evidently didn't want to be referred to by the disrespectful nickname of 'chrome dome'.

He was dressed in a sober navy suit with a very discreet narrow stripe, with a pastel pink shirt and lavender tie, and looked every inch the young country solicitor.

Having presented their credentials, the two detectives took a seat in the chairs on the other side of his desk, usually occupied by the firm's clients, and began their questioning.

Mr Dingwall confirmed that he and Robin Eastwood had been business partners for approximately five years; that he was aware of Mr Eastwood's sexual orientation, and that this did not bother him one bit. It was his ability as a solicitor that was pertinent to his job and that was the only criterion he used when he was choosing a partner.

About his visit to the house the previous day, he admitted that he had driven over on a whim, about someone he was seeing this morning, and about whom he just wanted a word with Robin.

As there had been no answer to the door, he wondered if he might be in the garden, it being a fine, light evening, and let himself in with his emergency key.

He had realised at once that there was something seriously wrong, and had first searched the downstairs, even going as far as to see if the householder might have fled and taken refuge in the garden shed, but to no avail. There had been no sign of him.

Re-entering the house, he had gone upstairs rather

gingerly, fearing that there may be an intruder still on the premises, and had discovered Robin's body in the first room he had entered.

Ascertaining that he was the only living person in the house, he then alerted the police to the situation, but had had to beg to be let go, as his wife had got to go out that evening, and he had promised to babysit when he got back from Fairmile Green.

'I noticed yesterday evening when we were there, that there were movement sensors in the house. Did Mr Eastwood have an alarm system, or were they just dummies?' asked Falconer. This sort of bluff was quite common now with householders not really wanting the expense of a real system, and believing that the dummies would deter potential burglars.

'No, they were real enough. Robin had some very valuable antique furniture in his house.'

'Had the alarm gone off when you got there and let yourself in?'

'Now you come to mention it, it hadn't. I never thought about it at the time, then later I thought he'd probably gone upstairs to have a soak in the bath or something, so it wouldn't have been set, would it, if that had been the case?'

'We've now discovered that he died sometime yesterday morning. I think that alters things a bit, doesn't it?'

'Morning? I say, that puts a whole new complexion on things. If he'd just got up, the alarm would have been set from the night before.'

'Quite so, sir, so how did whoever it was get in without setting the thing off?'

'That's a real puzzler, and I'm glad it's not me who's got to find the answer to it.'

'Quite so, sir.' Falconer could quite understand his

position. He just wished it wasn't him, either, who needed to solve the mystery of how the murderer entered the house.

With nothing else to question the solicitor about, and having ascertained that he and the deceased had enjoyed a very amicable professional relationship, although they did not socialise, naturally, the two policemen got up to take their leave of him, and he solicitously saw them to the outside door himself.

Getting back into their single car which, as usual, was Falconer's Boxster, as he now refused to travel in the ruin of Carmichael's venerable – and probably dangerous – old Skoda, they set off down the road to Glass House. How the Skoda got through its annual MOT, the inspector couldn't understand, but unless Carmichael was using a bent garage – and this was unthinkable, considering how upright the sergeant was – it must be basically sound.

After pressing their way firmly through the representatives of the press and television, they finally made their way to the front door and rang the bell with a hunted feeling, looking back over their shoulders in case they had been pursued by reporters with digital recorders and microphones.

When McMurrough opened the door to them, he had only just got in, but he had a look about his eyes that said he hadn't been sleeping well, and that he'd not had such an easy journey through the encampment more or less on his doorstep.

'Come in,' he invited them, then immediately followed this up with, 'I've heard. Isn't it ghastly? Poor Robin. Did they take much?' He made no comment at all about the media presence outside, but then to him, publicity was publicity. It may not be pleasant at the moment, but it was all, in the end, grist to his machine of keeping in the public eye.

'Give us a chance to get in first, Mr McMurrough.'

'Sorry. It's just that I was so excited. I've got to tell someone or I'll burst. I went to see the head of casting first thing this morning about a possible part in *Allerton Farm* – you know, the soap opera – and they said I'd be perfect for what they want, and they're going to send me a contract. Isn't that just fab? And she – the head of casting – drove all the way down to Market Darley just to interview me – a concession because of my tragic loss.'

'Congratulations, Mr McMurrough. You must be very pleased.'

'Then I find out about poor Robin.' His face fell, melodramatically. 'Who could have done this filthy thing?'

'We don't know yet, sir. We're still trying to figure out whether Bailey's murderer was after him, or whether you were the real target, as you seemed to be with the other attempts.'

'Oh, I've just remembered something I meant to tell you. You know when I was nearly electrocuted? Well, Bailey had left his dressing gown in my bathroom. I can't remember why, just now, what with all the excitement, but if someone got into the house to set up that electrical trap and the trip wire, maybe they thought it was his bathroom, and he was the real target after all.'

'That's a very interesting theory, sir. We'll give it due consideration.'

'Do, because the trip wire, the great lump of stone on the gate, and the electric shock could have been for either of us, couldn't they?'

'The spiked drink was a little more specific, though.'

'I'd left my glass on the table by the barbecue. It could easily have been assumed to be Bailey's, if whoever it was didn't see me put it down before I went into the house.'

170

'That's true. It's an aspect of this case that we'll have to think about very carefully, Mr McMurrough.'

'Would you two like a glass of champagne? I know Bailey's dead and Robin's been murdered, too, but I really must celebrate my being offered this part in *Allerton Farm*. It could be a real launch pad for me.'

'Not at this time of day, sir, and not given the current circumstances, but thank you very much for the offer.'

'Before we go back to the station, I just want to go and see how Darren Worsley is, after his ordeal yesterday. I still feel like a heel for arresting him, even if Jelly insisted I did it.

'We'll drive down. The weather's not so good today, and I should have brought a jacket,' he said to Carmichael. 'Then we'll get straight back to the station and see if there are any more reports in for us. We could do with a bit of a chin wag about this – try to put some of the pieces of the jigsaw together, to see if we can get an idea of what the picture is, on the box lid.'

Darren Worsley opened the door to them, somewhat closer to the state in which they were now used to seeing him. 'Come on in and have a drink,' he invited them, with all the alcohol-induced bonhomie of a drunk.

'Not just now, sir, but thank you for the offer.' People only seemed to want to shove alcohol down their necks today. 'I only wanted to see if you were all right after what happened yesterday.'

'All part of life's rich tapestry, Inspector, and it was about time I had a few hours sober, if only to check that I hadn't completely addled my brain with the booze. And it would seem that, stone cold sober, I am in perfect control of all my faculties, although God knows why, the way I abuse my system.

'And I must have some friends left. I found a bottle of

171

rather nice wine left on my doorstep not long ago, with a label attached saying "Drink and enjoy", which I intend to do when I throw together something to eat for my evening meal, even if I have left it a bit late for that – must put a lining on the stomach, you know.'

'We'll leave you in peace, then. I just wanted to check up that you were all right.'

'I'm as right as ninepence, as my old granny used to say, whatever ninepence is.'

Falconer and Carmichael got back into the car, both mulling over different aspects of recent events, to try to sort out if there was any connection between the deaths, and who had been the intended victim in murder number one.

Falconer was also perplexed at why he had felt so relaxed in Carmichael's busy, chaotic household, when the thought of sharing his own home, even temporarily, with just one other person, filled him with trepidation, and brought him out in a cold sweat.

He had not even made a murmur earlier, when the younger boy had run his toy cars up and down his arms and across the back of his head and his shoulders, and the older one had urged him to try playing Angry Birds on his game machine.

Even the little one, Harriet, had got in on the 'let's play with Uncle Harry' game, and had played happily for quite some time with the bows in his shoelaces, at one point even leaning down to chew them, and he had been as cool as a cucumber.

He would need to ponder his mental attitude towards his home, and why he shied away from letting anybody into it. He suddenly felt like a snail, a creature that had a shell for only itself, and would not – could not – tolerate any visitors.

And that reminded him: he had not phoned Heather yet

to arrange their next meal together. If he didn't do it soon, she'd get the hump, and he didn't want to be in her bad books, did he?

Chapter Thirteen

Tuesday
Market Darley

Halfway through the afternoon, Harry Falconer received an internal telephone call from Bob Bryant on the front desk, that there had been a call from the ambulance service, that they had been called in by a woman to an address in Fairmile Green to what had been described by her as an unconscious man.

He also warned them that there was a substantial media presence outside the station, and that he might be well advised to use the back entrance, if he wanted to avoid any chance of someone wanting him to make a statement. It would also make it easier for him not to let out the fact that there was something else deadly afoot in the same small village.

The paramedics had realised almost immediately that the man who had been reported as unconscious to them was, in fact, dead. As he was a young man for whom they could do nothing further in this life, they had immediately alerted the police to the situation, and the Force, thereby, had yet another corpse on its hands.

Alerting Carmichael that they were about to go out with a movement of his head, he took down the address: Lane House, Old Darley Lane, Fairmile Green. That was Darren Worsley's address; surely the man couldn't have drunk himself to death since they had last seen him, but the member of the ambulance crew said that there were no obvious wounds on the body.

'Worsley's dead,' he said simply, getting up for his desk and heading for the door.

'Any idea what happened?' asked Carmichael, as he folded his great length into Falconer's car.

'None as yet. Bob said he'd get Doc Christmas on his way, but the ambulance crew can't find any injuries obvious to the naked eye. Apparently it was his mother who found him.'

'Nasty for her,' commented Carmichael.

'Very. I shouldn't relish finding a member of my own family dead, no matter how little contact I have with them, and for it to have been her son must have been a devastating shock.'

'It's not right, a child dying before its parents; it's against nature.'

Fairmile Green

The ambulance had been moved back to the main road when they arrived, presumably to allow easy access down Old Darley Passage for other vehicles. The crew had remained at the house with the bereaved mother until they arrived.

Having handed Worsley's mother over to another service, the ambulance crew took their leave, free once more to pursue their professional duties. Mrs Worsley they found in an armchair, sobbing into a handful of tissues and moaning softly to herself, while the lifeless body of her son lay sprawled on the settee, a pathetic sight at which she was determinedly avoiding looking.

'Mrs Worsley,' began Falconer, after the two detectives

had introduced themselves, 'Is there another room where we could talk? This feels very unsuitable and cruel. You should not have to sit in here with the evidence of your loss in full view.'

'There's a table and chairs in the kitchen,' she informed them in a broken voice, before resuming her helpless sobbing.

'Come along, and we'll go there, because we do need to talk about how you found your son.'

She went with them docilely, and made a visible effort to pull herself together, once they had all taken a seat at the old pine table that took up so much floor space in the small room.

'He had to have a table in here,' she said, as if an explanation were necessary. 'There's no dining room, and he didn't have a lot of work surface in here for food preparation – that's a laugh. How much room do you need to pour a drink?

'Everything's such a mess. His father's never spoken a word to him, you know, since he told him what he was – one of those, you know. He took right against his own flesh and blood and cut himself off completely from him.

'He's a hard man, and he just didn't understand that it wasn't something that Darren had chosen for a lifestyle. He was born that way, or that's what I believe, anyway.

'I don't work Tuesday afternoons, so I always popped over with a bag of groceries for him. He wasn't much of a one for shopping, and he'd live off crisps and chocolate if I didn't bring him some meals for the microwave, because he couldn't cook at all, and I just can't see him being bothered to put a sandwich together.

'I know he used to drink far too much, and it looks like it's done for him now. He just didn't know when he was well off, with that Radcliffe bloke and a nice house and everything.

'He just had to blow it, and when the house was sold, he just spent the money on more alcohol, with no thought of putting a deposit on a little flat, so he still had a foot on the property ladder, even if it was just on a lowly rung.'

At this point, she seemed to have talked herself out, and she sat there staring at the table top, quite out of breath. She was a bulky woman, dressed in an unsuitable horizontally striped cotton frock and a washed-out blue cardigan, her hair already mostly grey, and scraped back into a tiny unattractive bun at the base of her neck.

'How did you get here?' the inspector asked her, realising she was in no fit state to drive.

'I came up on the bus from Carsfold,' she told him, blowing her nose in a most unladylike way.

'I don't think you should use public transport to get home. I'll call one of our cars for you. You don't want people staring at you and trying to guess what's upset you.

'I'll get one of my men to give you a lift in a vehicle where you won't be an object of curiosity. My sergeant and I will have to go back into the other room, but we'll be back, and I'll finish up any further questions I have while we wait for a car to arrive.'

Falconer assured her that they would return in a few minutes, and he and Carmichael went back into the living room to take a better look at the latest victim of what he was beginning to think of as 'The Curse of Fairmile Green'.

Darren Worsley looked perfectly at peace where he lay, as if he had just fallen asleep or slid into drunken unconsciousness, with not a care in the world. On the overcrowded coffee table sat a wine bottle with still a couple of inches of red wine left in it.

'Didn't even finish it off,' observed Carmichael. 'Look, there's a label round its neck.'

Falconer leaned down and twitched the label so that he

could read it. 'It just tells him to drink and enjoy. No name. And I remember now!' he exclaimed, clapping one hand to his forehead, and pulling a rueful face.

'When we called round to see if he was all right yesterday, he said he must still have friends because one of them had left a bottle of wine on his doorstep. He said something about there being a message on it, and neither of us thought anything of it.

'Well, you'll remember. You were with me. He even asked us in for a drink, and if we'd agreed and entered the house, we'd have actually seen this label: or maybe if we'd just listened a bit more closely to exactly what he was telling us, we might have come in and confiscated the wine because the label looked suspicious, with no sender's name on it.'

'You can't think like that, sir. Neither of us is in any way responsible for what he drank. Apart from his own co-operation in actually necking the stuff, the person responsible is whoever put what they did into that wine bottle, obviously intending him harm.

'And if they put so much of whatever it was in it, that it did for him before he'd even emptied the bottle, then I'd say the intention was homicidal.' Carmichael was feeling very protective of his superior officer.

'But he'd probably had lots of other booze before that. That's what probably tipped him over the edge.'

'That's still not your responsibility, sir, and we can't be sure of anything until after the post-mortem. That's what you'd tell me if I had said what you've just said. *I* don't feel personally responsible for what he chose to drink, and neither should you.'

'All I *can* say,' retorted Falconer, 'is, given all that's happened, including this latest death, if it is one of the neighbours, then we've got a homicidal maniac living in the village. The only connection between the three men is

178

their sexuality, and I'm praying that's not the reason they were killed.'

'If it isn't somebody local, then do you think they might have had a common connection in the "gay world", if such a thing actually exists?' asked Carmichael.

'Don't say things like that. Do you know how far that opens up the field of suspects? We could be years on this one case alone. Even for a multiple murder, that's a bit of a slog.

'But we do have two homophobic couples right here on the doorstep, so to speak: the Fairchilds and the Catchesides. Maybe we need a further word with those two pairs of lovelies.

'I also seem to remember that one of them offered a religious slant on homosexuality at first. That can get people really hot under the collar, and incite them to things they would never normally consider doing.

'Remember that first case Roberts ever worked with us? We – and he – know only too well how people can work themselves up into a state of religious hysteria, and then there simply *are* no rules.'

At that moment, the doorbell rang, and Carmichael admitted Doc Christmas, showing him straight into the living room.

'Hello, Harry. Another stiff for me?'

'Shhh! His mother's just through there in the kitchen,' Falconer whispered, pointing towards the doorway. Returning to a normal volume, he said, 'Right, Carmichael, let's get back to Mrs Worsley, to see if she's got anything to tell us that might be pertinent to this terrible situation.'

Mrs Worsley had, in fact, reverted to a sort of motherly/housewifely role, and had just made a pot of tea. 'I thought it would do us all good,' she said, her eyes no longer drowned in tears. 'We can drink it while we wait

179

for my lift home, which it's was very kind of you to arrange.'

As they sat back down round the old table, Falconer asked her about her relationship with her late son. 'He was always different, even as a kiddie,' she confessed to them. 'Never liked football, or any of those rough-and-tumble boys games that my husband loved to play with the other lads.

'Those two never seemed to have anything in common, and most of Darren's friends at school seemed to be girls, but not *girlfriends*, if you see what I mean. When he 'came out' to us that was my husband finished with him. It made me feel protective, though.

'When I was a kiddie, people like that had a very hard time of it; shunned by family and friends alike, and they usually had a hard time of it finding work, too.

'I thought it would be like that for my Darren, as well, but times have changed and, apart from his drinking, which just got worse and worse once he didn't have to work any more, he led as close to a regular life as he could, considering that he was sharing his bed with another man.

'He told Radcliffe that he was sacked from his job, but he wasn't. He left work because he didn't like the boring job he did, and felt life owed him a better lifestyle, and that was his downfall. If he hadn't given up work, maybe he wouldn't have drunk so much, and we wouldn't be sitting here contemplating his passing today.'

Falconer tried to interrupt, but she held up her hand to forestall him. 'It's his nan I feel sorry for. When our Darren moved in with another man, she said it was just a phase he was going through. She refused to believe that they shared a bed, and had this touching belief that they were just best mates, and probably spent their evening looking at girlie magazines together.

180

'She was as pleased as punch when he moved out and rented this house. Said he'd come to his senses at least, and that he'd soon find himself a girlfriend, and that then we could look forward to the sound of wedding bells. This'll just about kill her. He was her favourite, you know.'

Another summons at the front door announced that Mrs Worsley's ride home had arrived. As Carmichael went to answer it, she rose from her seat and headed for the door into the living room. 'I just need to say goodbye to my boy, for the last time,' she said, and the tears began again to roll down her cheeks.

Falconer tried to forestall her, in case Doc Christmas had him turned face down with a thermometer up his bum to check his rectal temperature, but she managed to slip through his grasp. Luckily, the doc was just doing up his bag, preparatory to leaving. He may have moved the body to examine him thoroughly, but he had returned it to the position in which the two policemen had found it, and all was well.

Mrs Worsley leaned over the shell of her son and, rather touchingly, kissed him on the cheek, murmuring, 'Good night, son, sleep tight. I love you.' Then she practically marched out into the hall, as if she couldn't wait to get out of the house, and called a brief goodbye over her shoulder, as she went through the door and back into the outside, everyday world.

'I reckon this one was some sort of poisoning – maybe alcohol, but I can't be certain until I've had my wicked way with him. There was certainly no violence involved, though. From what I can see, there's not a mark on him, not that I've had time to check all the nooks and crannies, if you get my meaning,' Doc Christmas informed them with his usual pragmatism.

'I think we'll just make those other two calls I mentioned earlier, and get them over with,' said Falconer, now in the car and heading back towards Smithy Lane, which was the official address for both couples he intended that they talk to again.

At Church Cottage, both Vince and Nerys were home, and it was Vince who opened the door to them, his face crumpling into a scowl as he identified who his visitors were.

'You'd better come in, but we can't give you too long as we'll be eating soon,' he said, as welcome, ushering them inside where the smell of frying was in the air – nothing healthy, then.

'I doubt whether the village grapevine has got the information to you, yet, but Darren Worsley from Old Darley Passage has been poisoned. Apparently someone left a bottle of wine on his doorstep, and it contained a little something extra that proved fatal.'

Although Falconer was jumping the gun a little, telling them this, he had no doubt that his suspicions would be confirmed once the wine had been analysed and the post mortem had been carried out.

'Nothing to do with us, if that's what you're thinking,' said Vince, defensively. 'Come in here a minute, Nerys; there's a couple of fellows here want to know if we killed Darren Worsley – you know, that poof that used to go with that fellow from Glass House that got killed.'

Nerys joined them, making the smell of a hot frying pan even stronger. 'That's nothing at all to do with us, but that's the third one of *those* dead now, and I don't call that a bad thing.'

'It's a bit of a result, actually,' added Vince, on firmer ground now that his wife had joined him.

'Do you know anything about a bottle of wine that was left outside his door? That's all I want to ask you, apart from where you were between the hours of eight a.m. and twelve noon on Sunday.'

'So you reckon us for that Eastwood chap as well? Well, I'll tell you this; we might hate the perverts of this world, but it's not our place to eliminate them. We just make our feelings known when necessary, and you can put that in your pipe and smoke it. If you want to discuss this any further, I'm afraid my solicitor will have to be present.'

The two detectives retreated at this threat. Falconer didn't want solicitors to be brought into things at this stage of the enquiries. It was much too early, and any suspicions they had were far too tentative to talk about arresting anyone – with the exception of that unfortunate incident on Saturday morning, which Chivers had insisted upon.

He still felt bad about that, and even worse, now the man was dead, and just hoped that the press never found out about it – they'd have a field day, and might even suggest that police persecution drove him to suicide. Oh hell!

'Come on,' he said, 'Let's get round to Woodbine Cottage and talk to the unlovely Fairchilds.'

At Woodbine Cottage they found that all three family members were currently in residence, even Rufus being back from college and not back out for the evening on the rampage with his mates.

The noise coming from the house drowned anything that Roger said in greeting; all they could see were his lips moving. Without trying to make himself heard to them he went to the foot of the staircase and bellowed, 'Shut that blasted racket off and get down here now, Rufus!'

There was no response at all to this stentorian order, so he went halfway up the stairs and repeated it, this time causing the deafening drum and bass to cease within a few seconds, and for Rufus to appear at the head of the stairs.

'What d'yer want now?'

'It's the police.'

'The pigs? Again? This is police harassment,' the teenager shouted down belligerently.

'Get yourself down here immediately, and you'll speak respectfully if you open your mouth at all, miladdo.'

Rufus mooched sulkily down the stairs, eventually to join his parents in the living room. 'What d'yer want now?' asked Rita, not best pleased to see them in her house again.

'We'd like to know what you were doing between the hours of eight and twelve on Sunday morning, and whether any of you has been in the vicinity of Old Darley Passage in the last couple of days.' Falconer was unspecific, because he suddenly felt that he was wasting his time.

'We know that young Eastwood's got his just desserts, but what's that about Old Darley Passage? Has one of the shirt-lifters there got his comeuppance at last?' Roger Fairchild was almost dribbling with anticipation to the answer of his unspeakable question. There seemed to be no room for 'live and let live' in this household.

'Mr Worsley has been murdered. Someone left him a poisoned bottle of wine on his doorstep.'

'Well, when you find out who did that, let me know and I'll buy him a pint.'

'The Lord abominates men who lie with other men,' contributed Rita, just to add even more to the distasteful atmosphere.

'And are you regular churchgoers?' asked Falconer, and was overjoyed at their reply.

'We go,' spat Roger, defensively.

'Not every week, but we go sometimes,' added Rita.

'Then you'll know the Christian advice on forgiveness, and heed the Church's teachings on tolerance of others and

184

loving thy neighbour.' Falconer trumped their ace with a victorious smile. 'Would you care to answer my questions before we go?'

When they left, he made hand-washing motions, so glad was he to get out of their company, that he actually felt sullied. Homophobia was alive and well and living in the villages, apparently in peace and tranquillity. There should be a law against it.

As they headed back towards Market Darley, Falconer spoke only once. 'What a week it's been, and it's only been five days.'

'Quite, sir.'

Back in their office once more, they updated their records, Falconer finally closing down his computer and sighing deeply. 'Carmichael,' he said in a world-weary voice.

'Yes, sir,' replied the sergeant, looking up and noting that the boss was preparing to go home, and taking the welcome hint.

'Tell me what you think about this. There were five gay men in that village – to our knowledge; there may be more – and, of those five, three have, so far, been murdered. Would it be perceived as prejudiced if I suspected one or other of the other two of being guilty, or is it more likely to be someone from their wider lives who is responsible?'

Carmichael sat in contemplative silence for at least thirty seconds, then he replied, 'Don't know, sir. We can think about that tomorrow. Kerry's doing lamb stew and dumplings tonight, and I've been thinking about it all day.' It was time for him to fill the tank again.

Chapter Fourteen

Wednesday
Market Darley

Falconer had spent the first thirty minutes of Wednesday morning at work in Superintendent Chivers' office, being lectured on the responsibilities of an inspector of police to his community at large, with particular reference to arresting someone when they were the obvious suspect.

As Darren Worsley had also fallen victim to the Grim Reaper, he had transferred his suspicions to Gareth Jones. 'He had a perfect motive for doing away with that first chappie – the one you said wore a wig. He'd had his ... boyfriend, if I must use such an expression, stolen from him, and was just exacting revenge on said *boyfriend*'s new partner – the one who had done the stealing in the first place.'

'So why was the solicitor killed?'

'Maybe he saw something, and had to be done away with. Maybe he's leading a double life, and his death's nothing to do with the first one.'

'And Mr Worsley? What was the motive for his death?'

'If the solicitor was leading a double life, maybe Mr Worsley saw something, or maybe ... I don't know, but there must be some explanation for this mass slaughter of the members of a minority group.'

'You don't suspect Chadwick McMurrough, then?'

'·You don't want to go there, Inspector. Appear to pick on a man in the public eye like that, and you'll bring down the press on all our heads, and we can do without that. You make sure you treat Mr McMurrough with kid gloves and, remember, from what I've read in your case notes, it was Mr McMurrough's life that was threatened in the first place.

'It can hardly be a celebrity whose own life was in danger who's going around carrying out these awful murders, can it? No, you keep well away from McMurrough, or we'll all be on the front page of *The Sun* and the *Daily Star*, for police harassment of a media darling.'

'But, we wondered if maybe the booby traps had been set for Radcliffe, and he was the real intended victim.'

'Utter balderdash. Why would anyone want to hurt Mr Radcliffe in his own home? What was he, in the great scheme of things? A director on a soap opera? Who on earth could have had a murderous grudge against him?'

'His ex-partner.'

'Don't talk rubbish. You know as well as I do that his ex-partner's dead.'

'But what if there's more than one murderer in this case?' Falconer was getting absolutely exasperated. 'Jelly' didn't mind who had done the killings, as long as the media wasn't brought in on Chadwick McMurrough's behalf. He felt the superintendent was practically handcuffing him, but he had a few lines of enquiry left that he had to carry out, which did not involve the new star of television talk shows.

He had a couple of phone calls to make on another case he was working on and wanted to catch up with DC Roberts and his lumpy mumps, then he'd pick up

Carmichael, and they could make their way back to Fairmile Green. He wanted to talk to Terry Watkins of The Goat and Compasses again, and he wanted to try to catch Gareth Jones at home, possibly on a lunch break.

When he wandered back to his office, however, he was stopped in his tracks by the sartorial disaster that met his gaze. Carmichael was already in residence. He sat hunched over his desk, totally unaware of the effect he was having on the inspector's sense of good taste.

'Where in God's name did you get that suit, Carmichael?' he asked, almost in awe of his sergeant's ability to appear to be in fancy dress without having any idea of how he looked to others.

'I found it in my granny's loft,' he replied, still unaware of Falconer's horror. 'She said it was my granddad's and I thought it looked rather cool.'

'But, it's a demob suit,' Falconer almost squeaked, looking at the wide chalk stripe and the obvious cheapness of the material. 'And where did you get that shirt?'

'That shirt' had a loud paisley pattern that screamed 'retro', but not in any trendy or nice way. It was an absolute horror, and the inspector had not yet had the courage to pay any attention to the man's tie.

'And you expect me to take you out with me in that get-up? You expect me to be seen in public along with you wearing those abominations?'

'You're just out of touch with modern fashion, sir,' replied the sergeant, with a gentle smile at what he considered his boss's out of touch state, a far as clothing went. He had ceased, over long familiarity, to notice how elegantly Falconer was usually dressed, and how fastidious he was about his appearance.

'If we weren't going to Fairmile Green, with Castle Farthing much too out of the way to call off in, I'd make you go home and change into something a little less

188

"shouty". That outfit screams as if it were suffering terrible torture; rather like what my eyes are going through just having to look at you, Sergeant.'

'That seems rather a harsh judgement, sir.'

'It's a vote for good taste and sanity. I mean, have you actually looked in a mirror this morning?'

'Of course I have.'

'And did Kerry make any comment on how you were dressed when you left home?'

'No.'

'Did she look at you?'

'Yes.'

'And did her face tell a story.'

'Look, sometimes she and I just don't share the same taste.'

'Sometimes I don't think you have any taste at all. We're off to Fairmile Green again. May I suggest that you, at least, don't wear the jacket when we're actually interviewing members of the public.'

'But the jacket covers the shirt.'

'I know, but the jacket itself is so awful, that leaving it behind is the most considerate option.'

'No skin off my nose.'

'And you can take that off as well,' said Falconer, pointing towards Carmichael's chest. Now he had seen the tie, and it was a seventies confection of the browns and beiges so beloved of that decade, with a representation of a barely clad female on the front of it.

'I suppose that is your dad's, as is the shirt?' he asked wearily.

'I found those in the loft too,' replied Carmichael in a slightly hurt voice.

The inspector thought Carmichael had outgrown his 'no

dress sense' madness when he left home on his marriage, and was no longer a prisoner of the 'first-up-best-dressed' necessity of living with several brothers, but the influence of his wife had not cured him either.

Lately he had been rather better on the dress front, but in his hope of a cure, Falconer, it seemed, had been sadly mistaken, unless this was a one-off aberration harking back to their early days together. He had his doubt the other evening, when they had to go to Fairmile Green together. Now, only time would tell.

Grabbing his sunglasses from his desk and putting them on before he left the office, lest he should be blinded by the mobile rainbow that was his sergeant, Falconer marched out of the office, a determined and brave expression on his face.

Fairmile Green

By the time they reached the village, the pub was already open – it started serving earlier in the summer months than in the winter, to maximise passing tourist trade, all of which helped to keep the landlord in the style to which he had become accustomed since all-day opening had been legally approved.

There were a few souls in the bar, but it was easy to order their drinks and corner Terry Watkins down at one end of the bar. 'I'm glad you two've come back. I was slightly less than honest with you the other day, and would just like to put you straight about things concerning young Eastwood. I will also say that I don't usually gossip about my customers, and I'd be grateful if you didn't tell anyone where you got the information I'm about to give you.'

'Is that so, sir? We'd be grateful if you would enlighten us, and of course we won't reveal you as a source.'

A slight air of tension had ensued, which Carmichael

completely shattered by asking for three packets of chicken-flavoured crisps. He hadn't eaten for a few hours and was peckish.

Handing over the rustling handful and taking the cascade of small change which he had received in exchange, Terry Watkins leant his bulk against the bar and began, in confidential mood, to pass on the information he had previously withheld.

'I told you young Eastwood used to come in here quite often for a drink towards closing time. I left you, I think, with the idea that he just liked a bit of fresh air before going to bed. Well, that's not quite the full story.'

'Really? What is, then?' Falconer's curiosity had really been piqued. Carmichael was too busy stuffing his mouth with crisps to take notice.

'You'll know by now that he was gay. He was also a risk-taker in life. His real reason for coming here – which I might say, was mostly in the summer months – was cottaging.'

'Cottaging?' exclaimed Falconer, totally dumbfounded at the thought of a pillar of the community indulging in such a practice.

'Co-mmphm-ttag-crunch-crunch-ing?' asked Carmichael, suddenly re-joining the real world around him.

'Eastwood? That dapper young man that we met?' Falconer was still in a state of disbelief.

'What's – mmphmmn – cottaging?' asked Carmichael, aware that some momentous news had been imparted, but unable to understand exactly what this was.

Falconer leaned over and whispered into his ear, while the sergeant's face became redder and redder, and his eyes began to bulge. Finally, he was moved to speech. 'No, sir. Never.'

Both Falconer and Terry Watkins nodded in affirmation

191

of what had just been passed on to him, and Carmichael very nearly choked on his crisps.

'The tourist trade was his main area of stalking, and that's why he came in fairly close to closing time; so that if there was anyone who was a little backward in coming forward, they would have had a few drinks by then, and be feeling a bit more relaxed and adventurous.'

'Did he have any luck the night that Radcliffe was killed?' Falconer asked, with some urgency in his voice. Whatever the answer, it could have some impact on what had happened, and might either point to his involvement, somehow, with the death of Bailey – maybe turned down, and took exception to it – or to his own death, with the return of whoever he had picked up.

'I don't think so, but I can't be exactly sure. Not too long after I'd served him his drink, a load of those fans of that young 'un down at Glass House came up for refills. The older man had left, and the young 'un had gone out to wave him off, so the fans from his table all rushed to get another drink in before closing time.

'It was while I was dealing with this sudden pre-last orders rush that Eastwood abandoned his empty glass and swanned off into the night, and I didn't actually see him leave with anyone 'on his arm', so to speak. No, with consideration, I don't think he'd found a punter that night.'

'And McMurrough came back to the bar? After how long?'

'I'd been struggling to recollect his name. Thanks for that, and he did come back after, oh, I suppose, a few minutes. I couldn't give you an exact time because I was still busy, it being everyone's chance to get one last drink in, and it being Friday night and all.

'And I was very glad when he and all his followers left. Not only was there a lot of noise from that table, which doesn't normally bother me, because this is a public house, but it was that little pseud's voice.

'Over and over again, I heard him say the same thing, and his voice is high-pitched enough to stand out in a crowd.'

'What was it he kept saying?'

'"And now back to me."'

Falconer cleared his throat to give himself the opportunity to bring the conversation back to where they had left it, before they went off on this tangent. 'And Eastwood never came back?'

'Nope. I reckon he realised he'd missed his chance that night.'

'You had Gareth Jones in as well, didn't you?'

'Just the quick look in, but I told you about that last time we spoke. He went off pretty sharpish, and no, he didn't come back later. If I'd been asked, I'd have said it was a fairly quiet night all round, except for that one table, and that nothing much had happened. I'd never have guessed that there had been murder done only a few steps from this licensed premises.'

'Is there anything else you can recall about any of the people involved in these three murders, that you think might be of use to us?'

'Not really. And the only thing that is of interest to me is that, now Darren Worsley's been done for, my takings are definitely going to go down. He didn't do all his drinking at home, you know; a lot of it he did in here, but that's tailed off recently.

'I suppose if we listen to those two old women, Mrs Gossip and Mrs Rumour, he'd got to the end of the money he'd got out of the house he used to share with Radcliffe, and was drinking more at home because it was cheaper.

'He still came in here quite often for an early one, which I reckon was purely for the chat. It must've been quite lonely for him, pouring booze down his neck, home alone, considering how a bit of the old 'merry juice' makes you want to talk non-stop.'

'Maybe he talked to the wall, like Shirley Valentine,' put in Carmichael, unexpectedly alerting him to the fact that he must have finished his multiple packets of crisps.

'I didn't think you'd have seen that film, Sergeant,' commented Watkins in surprise.

'Oh, I like old films. I saw it on the telly late one night, and thought it was really good, especially when she'd served her husband's steak to next door's dog. Made me think of Mulligan. He's a dog that lives a few doors from us. Did it remind *you* of him, sir?'

'I can't say that I've ever thought about it but, now you mention it, I can see the resemblance. Oh, excuse me a moment. There goes my mobile.' Falconer reached into his trouser pocket and extracted his phone, which was blaring out Alice Cooper's 'School's Out' in its idiosyncratic, tinny way.

Although he didn't set it on speaker, the hysterical voice on the other end of the line could easily be heard. The inspector held the instrument slightly away from his ear, as Chadwick McMurrough wailed out his tale of woe.

'I need you to come here at once, Inspector. I've been getting silent phone calls. And I do know someone's there, because I can hear them breathing. I heard about Darren, and this all started yesterday evening.

'I need you here for my protection, because I think I'm next. Whoever this is, is going to do for me next, I just know he is; I can feel it in my bones. Oh, get here as fast as you can, before I pass out in sheer fear. And see what you can do about all those reporters outside. Tell them they're causing an obstruction, or something else police-y. I need you here so I can feel safe.'

'And what do you suppose I can do for your safety,

194

sir?'

'Just being here will be good. We can talk about what you can cause to happen when you get here.'

'Well, you'll have to wait a little while. I can't just drop everything and run to your side. If you're in really urgent need of a police presence, I can get a patrol car to drop round to you, to keep you company until we arrive.'

The young star suddenly took a turn for the better, and said, 'Oh, don't be so melodramatic. I'm sure I'll survive, if you take a while to get here. Come through the side gate; I'm in the garden soaking up the sun – always so scarce in an English summer, don't you think?'

'OK, sir,' agreed Falconer, surprised at the chameleon-like quality of the young man's moods. 'We are actually in the village, but we do have another call to make, and we will need to get some lunch.'

At this, Carmichael pricked up his ears. Crisps are not really a satisfying snack, and with his large six-foot-five frame to maintain, his belly was beginning to think his throat was cut.

'Well, don't be too long.' The note of anxiety was back in the young man's voice again – how mercurial he was.

'I need to make the other visit, but we'll pick up something on the way, to save time. I notice there's plenty of choice of takeaway food down the two main streets.'

'I'm sure I can find a couple of fine bone china plates for you to use, although I don't know if I have one large enough for a meal for your sergeant. He is built on the big side, isn't he?'

Falconer ended the call quickly, not liking the tone of lechery that had accompanied this last sentence, and he didn't think Carmichael would appreciate being the object of desire of Chadwick McMurrough, no matter how big a fan of his he was.

He only hoped that McMurrough behaved himself

when they arrived. The man had been quite flirtatious with Eastwood on the very night that Bailey was murdered. He didn't much fancy spending the whole of their proposed visit to Glass House with its owner hungrily eyeing up his colleague.

They stopped the car halfway down the High Street and walked the few yards down Old Darley Passage to the house 'Or Not 2B' for a little chat with Gareth Jones. As the only other gay man, apart from McMurrough, left alive in Fairmile Green, maybe he could give them a different perspective on the case.

They interrupted him packing a suitcase, and Falconer enquired if he was going away on holiday. 'No, I'd hardly call it a holiday. This whole business has spooked me badly, and I'm going back to me mum's for a bit. I don't feel safe here any more. If you like, I'm running away, but at least that means I'm still alive, which is more than can be said for some.'

'You feel you might be in danger, then?'

'Definitely. Look at it from my point of view: apart from me and Chadwick, there were only three other men of our persuasion in this village – namely, Bailey Radcliffe, Robin Eastwood, and Darren Worsley. They're all dead – murdered. Now, this may not be a gay vendetta, and I'd be happy to be wrong about that, but I want to be still alive to actually have an opinion on it.

'I'll be safer at me mum's, and it's not too bad there. At least they accept me for what I am, which is more than Darren's father did. And I'll have me sister for company, if I want it. And she's not averse to accompanying me to a gay bar or two – she says she's probably a fag hag, but can't help enjoying the company of "queers", as she calls us.'

'Perhaps you'd be good enough to give DS Carmichael

here your forwarding address and a telephone number where we can contact you, should we need to speak to you again.'

'No problem,' replied Jones, and scribbled the details down on a page torn from a notebook that had been lying around, handy for just this sort of purpose.

Back out on the main drag, once more, Falconer scoured the parades of retail establishments on both sides of the road. 'Right,' he said, 'We've got the choice of a restaurant or a bakery on this side, or a sandwich bar or a burger bar, across the stream. What do you fancy, Carmichael?'

'Well, the restaurant's out, as we said we'd get something takeaway, and I don't think the burger bar would be a good idea either. I don't want to get grease and ketchup all over my dad's shirt, or my granddad's good suit trousers.' ('Good' wasn't exactly how Falconer would have described that particular item of clothing.) 'I think on the whole, we ought to discount the bakery, and call into the sandwich shop. They usually have a good selection these days.'

'Sandwich bar it is, then. Get in, and we'll go back towards the pub and down Market Street, then we can take the car straight down to Glass House, and join its owner in the garden, which I believe was where he said he was sitting. I must say, it really is quite warm today, isn't it?'

'Couldn't agree more, sir,' replied Carmichael, glad now, that he had taken off his jacket and tie. 'Shall I drive?'

As they had come out, as usual in Falconer's beloved Boxster, the answer was an unequivocal 'no', and the inspector was at the wheel as they made their way to the sandwich bar, which was halfway down Market Street.

Chapter Fifteen

Fairmile Green

They did as Chadwick had bidden Falconer, and entered Glass House's rear garden by way of the side gate. Stretched out on a sun lounger with a glass in his hand, and a small table by his side, they found Chadwick McMurrough who must have, just for a moment, forgotten to look terrorised.

Two other loungers had also been set out, evidently in anticipation of their arrival and, on a cast iron table with four chairs round it, stood an open bottle of champagne in an ice bucket and a jug of what appeared to be orange juice.

Hearing their approach, he sat up and immediately adopted a helpless expression, full of trepidation, suitable for one who went in fear of his life.

'Thank God you've arrived,' he said in a breathy and vulnerable-sounding voice. 'I've been so worried. Take a seat, do, and if that's your lunch in that carrier bag, then feel free to eat it. I'll go in and get you a couple of plates.'

As good as his word, he went into the kitchen, while the two detectives settled themselves at the table, this being a more suitable place to eat than on a sun lounger.

Within less than a minute, a fine-quality plate was set before each of them, and their host assumed his prone position on his lounger. 'Do excuse me if I carry on

198

catching the rays, only there's not much opportunity to do so in this country, so moody is its weather.'

It did not take the two men long to dispose of their sandwiches, and McMurrough immediately offered them a glass of Buck's Fizz to wash it down with.

'It's a bit early in the day for us to consume alcohol, and we don't normally drink while we're on duty, but if you have any lemonade, a lemonade and orange juice would be most welcome,' replied Falconer, taking real pleasure in uttering that old phrase 'not while we're on duty'.

Once again, Chadwick disappeared into the kitchen, and came out with two tumblers filled to the brim with the requested beverages. The two men moved over to the loungers to appear more sociable and put this particular witness at his ease.

'Do you mind if I lie down again?' asked Chadwick.

'You carry on, sir. But do tell us if anything else has come back to you since we last spoke, or if you've learnt anything that might be of interest to us,' urged Falconer as he and his sergeant adjusted the loungers to a more upright position suitable to the dignity of policemen about their lawful business.

A look of low cunning passed over Chadwick's face, before being replaced again by his innocent one. 'Did you know that Robin Eastwood was into rough trade?' he asked provocatively, accompanying his question with a little smirk of superiority.

'If you mean did we know he was cottaging, yes, we did, as a matter of fact. Do you think that has any bearing on things?' Momentarily, McMurrough looked surprised at their knowledge.

'I've been thinking,' the young man replied however, now looking slightly more serious. 'If he'd been picking up casuals, couldn't it have been one of those that did for him? It's a risky business, picking up complete strangers – and letting them into your homes, if you're really stupid. Even going up a dark alley with them isn't very clever. Anything could happen.'

'And your point is, Mr McMurrough?'

'Do call me Chad or Chadwick, please. And my point is, he could easily have been killed by one of his casual punters.'

'He was killed before he'd even got up.'

'So that has to mean that he went to bed alone, does it?' That gave both policeman pause for thought.

'I see what you mean. Oh, excuse me, there goes my mobile again.'

Falconer retrieved his phone again, got to his feet and began to wander around the garden, then he headed back to the metal table, extracted a tiny notebook from his trouser pocket, with a pencil down its spine, and began to make notes with one hand, while holding the phone between his jawbone and shoulder blade.

When he re-joined the other two, they had gone back to Bailey's murder, and McMurrough was suggesting something along the lines of what Terry Watkins, the landlord, had suggested.

'What if, as Eastwood obviously didn't manage to pick up any trade – how could he? The place was full of my fans, not his touristic prey – and he was miffed when he left the pub.

'What if Bailey had stopped to look at the stream or something like that – maybe into a shop window, although I can't think of any of them that would be of particular interest to him. What if he tried it on with Bailey, and got given the cold shoulder?

'Maybe he was so furious by then, obviously feeling horny, and not being able to find a partner, that he walloped Bailey one …'

'With what, sir?'

'I don't know, do I? Something he had about his person, I presume, and Bailey just fell into the stream and hit his head, or something, on the way in.

'And have you given any thought to my ex-partner, Gareth Jones? He might have done in Bailey because he thinks he stole me from him. Then, he might have got wind of Eastwood sniffing round me, and done the same thing again, purely out of jealously and spite.

'I can even come up with a motive for doing away with Worsley, too. Did you know the two of them used to have long cosy chats about us, which eventually turned into back-biting sessions? Perhaps Gareth confided things to him that he wished he hadn't mentioned, and wiped him out to prevent him using them against him.'

It was beginning to seem as if 'the lady' doth protest too much. McMurrough was certainly generous in the way he hurled around suspicions and accusations.

'Do you know that Jones has a dossier of photographs and other things about you that he intends to go to the press with?' Falconer suddenly interjected.

'There you go, then. He was preventing Worsley from selling his story first. The early bird gets the most headlines and column space, after all.'

'Don't you mind, Chadwick?' asked Carmichael, amazed at how cool the young man was, given what he had just been told.

'Not at all. There's no such thing as bad publicity. Anything that gets me into the rags is good for my career, and I don't begrudge Gareth the money. He works very hard as an electrician, and I don't envy him anything at all about his life. But I, personally, could make a very good case against him as the person responsible for these three deaths.

'I reckon you ought to take a good, long, hard look at

my ex-partner, and decide what he's really capable of. You might be surprised.'

The mention of Jones being an electrician gave Carmichael pause for thought, when he remembered the booby trap that had given McMurrough a nasty electric shock, but the man had appeared to be totally without guile or guilt when they had visited him a bit earlier, and he had mentioned his profession with no prompting when they had first spoken to him, without a trace of shiftiness in his manner.

Neither he nor Falconer had laid much importance on Jones' profession, so much had happened in this village, but maybe that had been an omission they should not have made.

Surely Jones couldn't have pulled the wool over their eyes so convincingly if he had three deaths on his conscience, but it would explain why he was packing a bag to go away. He'd have to have a quiet word with Falconer later, to see if he wanted to pay a return visit to Old Darley Passage. Carmichael mentally crossed his fingers that they had not both made a bad error of judgement.

A voice broke into his reverie. 'But that's enough about the past. Now, back to me.'

At that moment, Falconer's phone broke out joyously again into 'School's Out', and he momentarily walked off again for the sake of privacy. Once again, he circled back round to the table and wrote in his miniature notebook.

This time, when he re-joined the other two, they were talking about Darren Worsley's untimely death. 'That man would have drunk anything if it had a booze label on it,' Chadwick was declaiming, then went thoughtful for a moment.

'I hope you don't find it odd that I'm drinking champagne after yet another acquaintance's death, only I'm having another bit of a celebration about getting that part in *Allerton Farm* – a bit of a coup for me, that was.'

Carmichael, ever a fan, decided he wanted to know more. 'Wouldn't you rather have gone back into *Cockneys*, sir ... Chadwick?'

'Bailey was trying his best on my behalf, but he wasn't really getting anywhere, so I decided to cast my own net upon the waters, so to speak, and it came back with a live fish in it.'

'What about those other similar programmes?' Carmichael wasn't giving up until he had the ins and outs of a duck's arse. 'What about *Mafeking Street* – that's been running, like, for ever, and it's got very high viewing figures – higher than *Allerton Farm*, anyway.'

'Granted, but both *Mafeking Street* and *Cockneys* have a murderous filming schedule, as they go out with so many episodes a week, and I would like a bit of a social life left after work, if you don't mind.'

'OK, then, what about *Fouracre*?' asked the sergeant, with a smirk. It was a soap opera all about young people, and marketing directly at young people, almost a natural slot for McMurrough to try for.

Falconer's phone rang again, but the two younger men hardly noticed him leaving them once more to conduct his telephonic conversation.

'What, with all those youngsters about all the time – a lot of them even younger than me? I'd not only have to be looking my absolute best every minute of the day, but I'd need to employ someone full-time just to keep an eye out for crow's feet, grey hairs, and any other visible sign of ageing, like not wearing the latest fashions, or knowing what the latest drink is. Do you know what a Jager Bomb is, Sergeant?'

'No, and call me Davey, please.' I'll have one last try, he thought. 'What about *A&E*? That's got a good mix of ages in it, and it only goes out once a week, and has a sister show that you could move over to if they run out of stories for you in that series.' Carmichael watched a lot more television now that he was married, and most of what they watched was Kerry's choice.

'Smart choice, *Davey.*' Chadwick made great play of pronouncing Carmichael's forename with much emphasis, raising a smile of pride from him, that such a celebrity had actually used his first name (even if said forename was really Ralph and not Davey).

'I had seriously considered approaching the makers of *A&E*, and I haven't completely ruled it out. It just depends on the meatiness of the storylines I get given in *Allerton Farm*. If I'm just going to be along the lines of 'the only gay in the village', then they can stick the part, after I've investigated the possibilities of becoming a regular on the once-a-week show.'

'And now I must tell you about Jager Bombs – and Irish Car Bombs.'

'Waste of time, Chad. I don't really drink, and I've never really recovered from my first taste of tequila with a couple of my brothers. We did it the traditional way – salt on the space between the thumb and forefinger, slice of lime waiting.'

'I know,' chimed in Chadwick. 'You lick the salt, throw the shot of tequila down your throat, then bite the slice of lime. Tequila slammers, they called them, because you're supposed to slam down the glass as soon as you've necked the shot.'

'That's it. I passed out after only four shots – I even missed the table trying to focus enough to slam down my glass – and they dumped me on the sofa and carried on till they'd finished the bottle. I woke up the next morning with a mouth like the bottom of a budgie's cage and a feeling that I'd completely lost the evening.

'Hey, do you mind if I use your loo?' Carmichael

couldn't bear to use the word 'lavatory', but didn't like the sound of 'toilet' either. 'That orange juice has gone straight through me.' He was also conscious of the liquid he had consumed in the pub, and was beginning to feel desperate.

'Not at all. Through to the hall, then over on your right. You can't miss it. It's got a sign on the door that says "Little Boys' Room" .'

'Thank you very much, Chadwick. I'll be right back.'

As Carmichael disappeared into the house, McMurrough began enquiring of Falconer if he knew about Jager Bombs and Irish Car Bombs. The inspector let him ramble on about how to make these two explosive drinks while he digested what he had learnt from the three calls he had received on his mobile since they had arrived here. There was certainly a lot of food for thought to get through, and he rather hoped that Carmichael wouldn't hurry back. He had a lot to digest, and could leave McMurrough to witter on in his egotistical way for as long as he saw fit to. The odd nod of the head should keep him happy.

Carmichael was just entering the kitchen, on his way back to the garden, when he suddenly thought it would be nice to have some ice in their next drink, as they weren't planning to leave in the near future, and he'd rather been enjoying himself, talking to someone who regularly appeared on TV and in the gossip columns.

He caught sight of a glass bowl on the work surface, and picked it up as a worthy vessel in which to carry ice, then he approached the upper half of a fridge freezer and opened the door.

Hello, whatever was a mobile phone doing in the freezer, hidden under the ice-cube bags like that? And what else was in here? He'd never seen anything like that before, he thought as he took out what looked exactly like a giant match with a metal head. It didn't look like a kitchen tool at all, but perhaps his new friend Chadwick used it to break up the ice.

Slipping the phone in his pocket, he went outside again, bowl of ice in one hand, and brandishing the strange giant match-shaped thing in the other.

Falconer was, once more, sitting at the metal table, and saw his sergeant emerge, and what he held in both hands. McMurrough was lying on his sun lounger, still droning on about the recipes for the most hip cocktails on today's scene.

Falconer's eyes stood out of his head in surprise, and he rose as soundlessly as he could, and signalled to Carmichael to keep silent, while getting an evidence bag out of his brief case.

'I only went to get some ice, sir,' said Carmichael, in direct disobedience of a mimed order from a superior officer, but he hadn't given the game away yet. Falconer signalled for him to put the mystery object into the bag, then put it into his case, a finger to his lips, to indicate a return to the previously sought silence.

McMurrough stirred slightly on his lounger and asked if Davey would mind pouring them all another drink. That was the end of a relaxing interlude.

'I found something in your freezer, Chadwick,' the sergeant suddenly announced, once more breaking an order, and moving McMurrough to try to struggle to his feet.

'Stop him, Carmichael! Don't let him get away!' shouted Falconer. For a few seconds, Carmichael looked at a loss at what to do, having no understanding whatsoever of Falconer's urgency in this matter, but it certainly drove all thoughts out of his head about paying a return visit to Gareth Jones.

'Sit on him, man! He mustn't escape!' shouted Falconer, now sounding desperate to detain McMurrough. 'Carmichael – SIT!' It worked for dogs, didn't it?

Out of sheer desperation and a sense of professional loyalty, Carmichael sat – like a good doggy.

Falconer called for a patrol car.

Chapter Sixteen

Market Darley

McMurrough was taken to the police station in Market Darley, and Falconer saw him through the booking-in process.

'So you'd given up on it being one of the neighbours, had you?' asked Carmichael, once they were back in the office and preparing to question, what Falconer was now convinced, was the murderer.

'If I hadn't, those phone calls I got while we were at Glass House would have been the final nail in the coffin of one of the neighbours being responsible. And now there had been three murders, it seemed too unlikely that we were looking for more than one murderer. The odds against that happening must be phenomenal.'

'What were the phone calls about, sir, and who were they from? There were three, if I remember correctly.'

'Spot on. The first one was from Doc Christmas about the blood tests on Worsley. He found ketamine again, and he said there was enough in his bloodstream to have killed a bull elephant. Someone wasn't taking any chances of him surviving.'

'What made you think of McMurrough in connection with that information?'

'Just that he moves in the sort of circles where drugs

can be obtained easily. He frequents television studios and night clubs. The things are available in those sorts of places, and he had quite likely taken advantage of that availability, to aid him in his tangled scheming.'

'And the second phone call?'

'Now that was interesting. It was a report from forensics about stains found on the rug in Robin Eastwood's house. You remember how it was almost all parquet flooring, with just the odd – and expensive, I might add – rug scattered here and there?'

'Rather cold, I thought that. I like my fitted carpets, especially in the winter.'

'Quite,' replied Falconer, who also liked his comfort. 'Anyway, there were some small stains on the rug at the bottom of the bed, where the body was found, and samples were taken, in case they proved relevant to our investigation. It only turns out that they were peacock poo.'

'No!'

'Yes, and who was the most likely person to have carried peacock excreta into his house, other than McMurrough? How suspicious, then, that the stains were on the rug in the bedroom. They must have got there when he stabbed him.'

'And the third call, sir?'

'That was the most interesting of all. It was about the fingerprint on the bottle that contained the spiked wine that killed Worsley – God, this is getting to be like 'The House that Jack Built'. I expected only the victim's fingerprints to be on it, but there proved to be a perfectly clear thumb print of a second person, as well; one which our guys were able to identify from those we took for elimination purposes. Guess whose?'

'McMurrough's?' As Carmichael had been listening to the inspector's explanation of his telephonic communications, he had also removed the phone he had found in the freezer at Glass House from his pocket, and was absent-mindedly playing with it.

'Absolutely right.'

'What was that thing I brought out to you that looked like a giant matchstick?' asked the sergeant, the object in question brought to mind because of the presence of the mobile phone.

'It's called a priest, and it's used by fishermen to knock their catches on the head with once they've landed them.'

'Didn't Radcliffe go fishing?'

'He did indeed and I think, if there are any prints on it at all, they will prove to be McMurrough's, although we could do with some more concrete evidence to strengthen the case against him.'

As he finished speaking, there was a strangled yell from Carmichael which, in more refined circles, would have been a cry of 'Eureka!' – I have found it!

'What is it, Carmichael?' asked Falconer. What are you playing with there?'

'It's a smartphone. I found it in the freezer at Glass House, too. I just put it in my pocket and forgot all about it, what with the excitement of the arrest and everything, I only just got it out to look at it.'

'So, what have you found?'

'It's only a photo of McMurrough actually wielding that matchstick thing. It's photographic evidence of the first murder.'

'Hallelujah!' replied Falconer, acting completely out of character and doing a little dance of triumph round the office. 'I'll get down to our little celebrity now, and see what he has to say for himself. I wonder why he didn't just throw the phone away.'

'Somebody would have found it and taken a look at it.

Even if he'd smashed it up, there's no telling what the geeks could get out of its remains.'

'And it survived being in the freezer. That's top marks for the manufacturers, then. Log it in as a piece of evidence, and we'll go and get our Mr McMurrough put in an interview room for us.

'At least we've got a motive for him taking out Eastwood now. I smell blackmail, even though I got the impression, the night Radcliffe was killed, that they were flirting, when we went to the house afterwards.'

DC Roberts chose that exact moment to phone, to ask if they'd thought of Radcliffe's partner as his murderer, the closest person to the victim often being the culprit.

'You're spot on, Roberts, but a little bit too late, I'm afraid. We'd already worked it out for ourselves,' Falconer informed him, not quite truthfully. 'Better luck on the next case, when you're back in the office on active duty.'

McMurrough was a skinny, hunched bundle on the hard chair in the interview room, looking faintly ridiculous in his trendy outfit. No longer did he appear as an up-and-coming soap star, but more like a little boy in fancy dress.

When Falconer and Carmichael entered the room, he didn't even bother to turn round, but merely swivelled his eyes in their direction. There was no hope in them. That had died back there, in the garden of his pretentious house, where, fortunately, no peacocks roamed any more. They, at least, had been taken care of, and carted off to more suitable accommodation than a private garden.

Falconer put the usual information onto the tape recorder when he started the recording, as to date, time, and those present in the room. 'Would you care to tell us about the death of your partner Bailey Radcliffe, Mr McMurrough?' he asked.

'For the tape, Mr McMurrough is not answering the

211

question,' Carmichael intoned in a serious voice, now that his latest hero had seriously blotted his copy-book.

'We also have Mr Eastwood's smartphone, so you now know we have photographic evidence that it was you who killed him,' Falconer pressed him.

At that, the apathetic figure raised its head and glared at them. 'It's all over, then?' it asked.

'It's all over, Mr McMurrough, but it will be considered as in your favour if you make a clean breast of things right now, before this thing drags on any further.'

For nearly a minute, the only sound in the room was the sound of the recording equipment, then Chadwick seemed to shake himself, moved to a much more upright position, and looked at the two men opposite him squarely.

'OK, you've got me for that.'

'We've also got forensic evidence that you are also responsible for the deaths of Mr Eastwood and Mr Worsley, so you might as well tell us the whole story.'

This was a little exaggerated, as they only had evidence of his presence in Eastwood's bedroom, and of him having handled the bottle of wine that killed Worsley, but they needed to shake him somehow.

That shook McMurrough, and for a moment, his shoulders slumped and his mouth gaped open, while his eyes registered, first horror, then hopelessness.

'I suppose it was inevitable, with the way things are now forensically. If I wanted to be a master criminal, I should have lived in the times the Sherlock Holmes stories were set. I suppose I'd have been a music hall star with my eye on the new medium of moving pictures, back then in the early days of the twentieth century.' This analogy raised a faint smile from him.

'You're quite right. I was responsible for all three deaths.' Got the little sod! 'Bailey's was something that never seriously crossed my mind until the actual day it

212

happened, and it felt absolutely crazy, once I'd done it. From then on, it was just one continuous nightmare.

'I thought Bailey could get me back into *Cockneys* and, at first, our age difference didn't seem to matter. Remember, before *The Glass House*, I was having a relationship with an electrician, and when I met Bailey on the set of *Cockneys*, he seemed to know so many people, and represented a glamorous world I'd only previously dreamed of.

'I thought if he could get me back into *Cockneys*, on top of my own chat show, that would cement my success for the future. But I credited him with more clout that he really had, and he couldn't actually do anything for me. It was something that took a little time to dawn on me, and that made him of no use at all to me.

'That was when I noticed what an old fogey he really was, with his wig and his fishing. I'm young. I should've been out with young people, having the time of my life, instead of living in an obscure little village with a man old enough to be my father.

'I began to resent him, and I sort of casually put that priest thingy into my man-bag before we went out that night. When he left to go home early, and I went out after him, I swear killing him was a completely spur of the moment thing.'

'But you, nevertheless, took it with you when you went out together for a drink.'

'That was no different from a married woman having a bank account in her name only, in addition to the joint one she shares with her husband. It gives her a feeling that she's free to break out, if ever she wants to. That was how I felt with the presence of the priest in my bag, only I took it one step further, and actually used it.'

'And all those "attempts on your life"? That was you, too, so there must have been an element of premeditation.'

213

'It started out as a bit of a publicity thing, then I saw how it could work to my advantage, but not until the night of the actual murder, and the mistaken identity thing was just to further muddy the waters. I mean, all those random attempts could have been aimed as much at Bailey as at me. It could just have been coincidence that I was the one who got hurt and, I assure you, I really did get hurt.'

'I don't doubt that for one minute, but let's go back to the night that you attacked Bailey Radcliffe, Mr McMurrough.'

'He didn't suspect a thing when I came up behind him and said something. He didn't even turn round, which was another reason why I did it. His head was almost asking to be clubbed.

'Then, I'm ashamed to say, that I pushed him into the stream with my foot. He was still alive at that point, but it was easy enough to hold his head down under the water, using my foot again, as he was barely conscious, and not strong enough to struggle.'

'What was going on back home, when we came round later and found Robin Eastwood with you?'

'I'd given him a ring as I knew he'd have some fags, as I told you at the time. I'd only met him briefly at our party, but I could tell immediately that he was 'one of us', and I just thought it was a kind thought which may have had something to do with my fame – it must count for something, after all. And he actually started to flirt with me. He'd already given me the eye at the party.

'Well, I'm not one to pass up a free lunch, so I twinkled back at him and thought, if this is the direction my life's going to take for a while, it'll at least give me breathing space to get settled into my new part on *Allerton Farm*.

'Then you two arrived, and I answered your questions as best as I could, thinking on my feet as quickly as I could, and I don't think I did too bad a job of it, even if I say so myself. I am, basically, an actor, you know.'

'Anyway, that's getting off the subject a bit. When you left, he came out with his real reason for coming round. He must've guessed you'd need to pay me a visit, and timed everything for when you'd been and gone for the day.

'Without any preamble, he just whipped out his phone and showed me the evidence he had – "in living and not-so-living colour", as he put it. Then he put on the thumbscrews. I was to be his swain, and line his pockets at the same time. He wanted an entrée to the clubs and any showbiz parties I was invited to – huh! That'll be the day – and I was his ticket to showbiz and the beautiful people.

Still, being an actor, I repressed my repulsion, and told him that, apart from lunch on Saturday, to which he was invited, that I didn't have any free time until Sunday morning.

I'd probably have to spend quite a lot of time talking to you in the meantime but, if he wanted me to, I'd call round first thing that morning, and I still kept up my act of flirting with him, saying that a relationship with him would be wonderful, and that, of course, I'd be willing to share the good fortune of my earnings with him.

'What a plonker! He only went and gave me a key and the code for the burglar alarm. It was like taking candy from a baby, and I knew that Bailey had at least one ferocious knife that he used when he went fishing. He unwittingly provided the weapon for both the first two murders.'

'And Mr Worsley? What did for him?'

'I saw him staggering around the night I ... killed Bailey. I was fairly sure he wouldn't remember a thing about it if he'd actually seen anything, but I realised I just couldn't risk it. A drunk's memory is a strange thing, and sometimes scenes just come back to them out of a clear blue sky.

215

'It was my belief that, if he did suffer from recall, he'd be onto me like a leech, to fund his booze habit and God knows what else. There was no way I could risk that, and I didn't think he'd be much of a loss to anybody.'

'Except his mother. She found his body, you know? How do you think your mother would have felt, if that had been your body?' Falconer had kept his silence for quite a while, but he felt he had to say something at this juncture, even if just to give the young man a bit of perspective on what he'd done.

'And I'm sure Bailey had family and friends who will miss him, as will Eastwood. Did you give any of those people a thought when you carried out these heinous crimes?'

'No. I only thought about me. I usually did, as everything seemed to be all about me. I was the one who was on the television. I was the one who was famous. Why shouldn't everything revolve around me?' McMurrough had recovered some of his customary arrogance when mixing with ordinary members of the public for whom he held no admiration or had no respect.

'Except the world doesn't work that way, Mr McMurrough. In the *real* world, our actions have *real* consequences, and I'm very much afraid that, after what you've done, one of the consequences is that you will be prosecuted and locked away in prison for a very long time.

'Should you live to be released, and pursue your interrupted acting career on the back of selling your story to the gutter press, I suggest that you will have to audition for much more mature, if not to say *elderly*, parts.'

McMurrough suddenly burst into tears of self-pity, and resumed his hunched position, sobbing loudly, at his tragic situation.

'May I suggest you give your solicitor a call? I'm surprised you didn't do that as soon as we arrested you?'

216

'It hardly seemed worth it. I didn't think you'd have considered bringing me in, if you didn't have sufficient evidence to take me to court.'

You have no idea, buddy, how recent some of the evidence is, thought Falconer, catching Carmichael's eye and exchanging a knowing look in memory of their late find on Eastwood's camera. 'I'll get you to a telephone before you're returned to your cell, sir,' he said, unable to feel any empathy towards the young man.

'What about those silent phone calls you phoned me in such a panic about?'

'I told you I was an actor, Inspector. I was acting. I'm really pretty good, don't you think?'

There was silence in the room – a dumbfounded silence.

McMurrough had had it all, and he still wanted more. Not content with winning *The Glass House*, he wanted a partner who was connected with television. Not content with Bailey as his partner, he had wanted him to manipulate him, somehow, back into *Cockneys*.

Not content with his older partner, he wanted someone younger. Not content with his chat show, he wanted a part on *Allerton Farm*. Not content to share his money with a blackmailer, and not being able to go to the police, as said blackmailer had evidence that showed he was a murderer, he had killed him, too.

And not content that there was someone else out there who might be able to blow the gaff, and who was a blabber-mouthed alcoholic, he had killed a third time, to secure his own security in his personal, celebrity-fuelled little world.

And now that world had come tumbling down around his ears. Well, 'as ye reap, so shall ye sow' thought Falconer, who had attended Sunday school as a child, and church, first as a boarding school pupil, then as a member of the armed forces.

He was a great believer in taking responsibility for all of your actions, because they all came with consequences, all of which couldn't just be ignored and swept under the carpet.

Young people, in general, today, were great at just sweeping everything under a carpet, if it didn't fit in with their idea of themselves. It was all right to get blind drunk and vomit, urinate, or get into a fist fight in the street. It was all right to take drugs and do the same sort of thing. It was all right to take no birth control precautions and sleep around.

All of this sort of behaviour was *all right*, as long as it didn't ruin their lives in any way. Well, it wasn't all right in Falconer's book, and he felt that Carmichael would probably be of the same mind as him. Self-respect, and the ability to say no and mean it, had been lost by today's generation of young people and, in his opinion, society in general was the worse for it.

And the language! And the drunks were causing a problem even in the small town of Market Darley on a regular basis at the weekends in the small hours. The fights were a constant problem, as were unconscious bodies, unspeakable acts in the streets and shop doorways, and serious abusive harangues – and that was just the girls.

God only knew what condition their livers would be in when they actually grew up, if they lived that long. And to think that he used to think that the squaddies were foul-mouthed. Life still had a lot to teach him, although he'd been unaware of this at the time.

Falconer was interrupted in this composition of a moralistic sermon by the voice of their detainee. 'Do you think I could phone my agent as well?'

This was just as well, this bringing him back to earth, as he was in danger of slipping into a very pompous mood, and he could be very superior when this happened. And this interruption to his musings meant that he didn't burst into a lecture on young people, leaving Carmichael to burst his bubble (which he undoubtedly would have done instantly), and, thus, he retained his dignity.

He knew he had high standards – although he considered this only normal – and he did his best to stick to them. He was thoroughly fed up, both with the state of the world and the sheer gall of the recently apprehended killer.

And all that slogging away, interviewing the obnoxious villagers – and yet they only had the crucial evidence on their man because Carmichael had wanted a bit of ice in his drink …

When they got back to the office, Falconer's only comment, spoken in sour tones, was, 'You mark my words, Carmichael, that young man's going to be splashed all over the tabloids for some time to come. If nothing else, he's going to ensure he builds up a nice little nest egg for when they eventually let him out of prison; but if it was me, I'd throw away the key.'

'If it was me, I'd probably lose it,' replied Carmichael, now thoroughly disillusioned about his former media and television hero. 'I hope someone looks after that little dog of his.'

After a light meal of steamed salmon, salad, and new potatoes, Harry Falconer was relaxing with a glass of white wine surrounded by his cats, who had come in from the excitement of the outside world because the weather had turned from fair and warm to stormy.

He had the lights already on, as the sky had turned black with heavy clouds, and the first fat drops of rain were starting to fall on an evening made chilly by the drop in temperature from this cloud cover. The lid was back on the landscape, and mere man was at the mercy of the elements.

An unexpected ring on the doorbell forced him to put down the book he was reading, and he went to answer it in quizzical mood, for he wasn't expecting any visitors. Checking through the little window beside the door, he recognised Carmichael's huge frame, and immediately put his hand to the doorknob to let him in.

As he greeted him, the sergeant's body was convulsed with an enormous sob, and he tottered into the hall with tears running down his face. 'Whatever's the matter with you? Have you had bad news, or are you just upset about your favourite chat show host?'

This wasn't really an appropriate question, more a flippant one, but the inspector had no way of dealing with what was evidently very strong emotion.

'Come on in and sit down, and I'll get you something to drink.'

Carmichael staggered blindly into the living room, his huge lumbering form and the noises of distress coming from it spooking the cats, which immediately took flight *en masse* for the cat flap. Better the elements and relatively harmless drops of rain that whatever monster had just invaded their home.

The huge, shambling frame of the man collapsed on to the sofa, and his drowned face looked up at Falconer. 'Oh, sir,' he whimpered.

'Whatever's the matter with you? You know you can tell me anything. I'm the soul of discretion.'

'Oh, sir,' Carmichael repeated again and his body was wracked with a further storm of tears.

'Come on, tell me, then you'll feel a bit better, and we can work out what to do together.' Falconer was getting really worried, now. He'd never seen his colleague like this before. Something must have really got to him for him to end up in this sorry state.

'I-I'm not c-c-crying because I'm s-sad,' Carmichael managed to stutter. 'I-m c-crying b-b-because I'm h-happy.'

'You're in this state because you're *happy*?' Falconer was dumbfounded. 'Whatever has happened to make you this happy – this ecstatic? Have you won the lottery?'

'B-better than that, s-sir.' Carmichael was slowly pulling himself together. 'Kerry's expecting again, and the doctor thinks it might be twins. I wanted to come over and tell you face to face. You will be their godfather, won't you?'

It was now Falconer's turn to sit down heavily. Whatever next?

THE END

P.S. Dipsy Daxie was taken in by Daphne, one of the crew on *Chadwick's Chatterers*, and he soon became accustomed to a fine life of dainty morsels, soft cushions, and regular opportunities to romance canines of the opposite sex …

The Falconer Files – Short Stories
Andrea Frazer

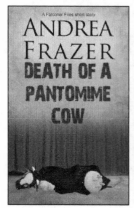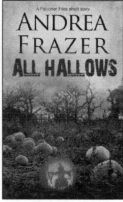

For more information about **Andrea Frazer**
and other **Accent Press** titles
please visit

www.accentpress.co.uk